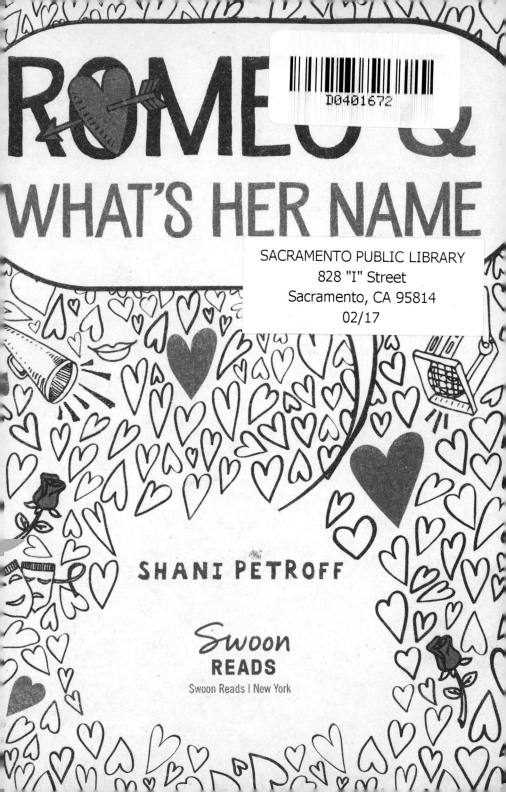

ROMEO & WHAT'S HER NAME

SHANI PETROFF

Swoon READS

Swoon Reads | New York

A Swoon Reads Book

An imprint of Feiwel and Friends and Macmillan Publishing Group, LLC

ROMEO & WHAT'S HER NAME. Copyright © 2017 by Shani Petroff. All rights reserved.

Printed in the United States of America by LSC Communications US, LLC (Lakeside Classic), Harrisonburg, Virginia

For information, address Swoon Reads, 175 Fifth Avenue, New York, N.Y. 10010.

Our books may be purchased in bulk for promotional, educational, or business use. Please contact your local bookseller or the Macmillan Corporate and Premium Sales Department at (800) 221-7945 ext. 5442 or by e-mail at MacmillanSpecial Markets@macmillan.com.

Library of Congress Cataloging-in-Publication Data

Names: Petroff, Shani, author.
Title: Romeo & what's her name / Shani Petroff.
Other titles: Romeo and what is her name
Description: First Edition. | New York : Swoon Reads, 2017. | Summary: "An unprepared understudy is forced to take the stage with her secret crush in this romantic comedy of errors"—Provided by publisher.
Identifiers: LCCN 2016015522 (print) | LCCN 2016036744 (ebook) | ISBN 9781250111142 (paperback) | ISBN 9781250111135 (ebook)
Subjects: | CYAC: Love—Fiction. | Theater—Fiction. | Schools—Fiction.
Classification: LCC PZ7.P44713 Ro 2017 (print) | LCC PZ7.P44713 (ebook) | DDC [Fic] —dc23
LC record available at https://lccn.loc.gov/2016015522

Book design by Rebecca Syracuse

First Edition—2017

10 9 8 7 6 5 4 3 2 1

swoonreads.com

FOR MY NEPHEW AND NIECE, LIAM AND
ALICE PETROFF, WHO HAVE STOLEN MY
HEART. ALWAYS KNOW YOU ARE SO VERY LOVED.

1

"What's so urgent?" my best friend Jillian Frankel called out as she made her way through the throngs of juniors clogging the halls of Shaker Heights High School.

I didn't answer. I couldn't. Not with so many spying ears around. I just waved at her to hurry up and get to Kayla's locker. I had news, and if I didn't spill it soon, I was going to burst.

"Well," Kayla Nunez, my other BFF, said when Jill finally made it over, "are you going to tell us?"

I looked around to make sure no one else was listening. "It's finally happening. I'm 99.9 percent sure *you know who* is single now!"

I didn't need to explain who I was talking about. They had both heard me go on and on about Wes Rosenthal enough to know I clearly meant him. Those giant brown eyes, that little dimple in his right cheek that's so deep you just want to poke it, the chiseled jawline that ought to belong to a Disney prince, those muscles that only come from playing lacrosse a million hours a week, that magical laugh you wish iTunes sold so you could play it over and over, the way he makes you feel as if you're the only person in the world who matters when you talk to him. . . .

"No way!" Kayla said, bringing me back from my Wes-dream. "Are you sure? Jace didn't say anything."

Jace Brennan was Kayla's boyfriend. He was also on the lacrosse team with Wes and one of his closest friends.

"Did Wes say something at the bus stop to make you think this?" Jill asked.

She was always so practical. I shook my head. "He wasn't there today."

"Ahhh," she said, leaning back on Kayla's locker. "That's why we got the SOS to meet *here*."

I gave a sheepish smile. "Her locker is more central." But they both knew the truth. I preferred the view. Kayla had been blessed with a locker directly across from Wes's. Like a true best friend, she offered to switch with me, but I didn't want to seem too obvious, so I kept mine, which was basically in the arctic of the junior locker hallway. "Okay, fine, I wanted to see Wes. If I don't get my bus time, I have to wait until last period to really get a chance to be around him."

"Maybe he's not coming in today," Kayla said.

"It's the first day back from winter vacation. He wouldn't miss it."

She shrugged. "Didn't you say he was away? He might not be back yet."

"He's back home."

Jill raised an eyebrow at me. "And how do you know that?"

"Okay, I know I promised I would stop stalking him online, but I couldn't help it. He's so cute, and I found out some really important stuff this time. *And* it's not *really* stalking, because we're friends. He follows me back."

Jill gave me one of her you-know-better-than-that looks. And she was right. I looked at Wes's GroupIt page way too much. It wasn't helping me get over my crush, and he was taken. At least he was—until now.

"What did you find?" she asked. "How do you know he's single?"

"Well," I said, trying to contain my excitement so I wouldn't cause a scene, "sometime between when I went to bed last night and when I woke up this morning, he took down all his pictures with *her*."

Her was Wes's girlfriend, Leora. They met at the summer camp they both worked at. She lived a few towns over. I never met her, but I kind of felt like I had because of all my snooping. We all did because I talked about her so much.

Kayla grabbed my arm. "He definitely wouldn't have done that if they were still together."

I squeezed my purse to my chest. "I know! Good-bye, Leora Zeltser. Hello, Emily Stein. This is my chance. I mean, I'm totally his type. I even look a little like Leora."

Both Kayla's and Jill's faces scrunched up. Okay, Leora was short, had dark eyes, a sleek pixie cut, gigantic boobs, an oval face, and delicate features, while I was average height, with a round face, massive blue eyes, and fairly frizzy hair that went just past my shoulders.

"Well, maybe if you squint just right," Jill offered.

"And you both have brown hair," Kayla added.

"But it doesn't matter," Jill said. "It's better that you're not alike. If he wanted her, he'd still be with her. He's moving on."

"Unless she dumped him," I said. I hadn't really considered that before. It seemed kind of crazy to think someone would dump the hottest, sweetest, nicest guy in the whole state of Ohio, possibly even the country, but stranger things had happened. "What if all he can talk about is how much he wants her back?"

"Now's your chance to find out," Kayla said, her eyes focused about twenty feet away.

It was Wes, and he was making his way toward us, or rather, his locker.

Relax, I instructed myself. I tended to get flustered around him. About half the time I was a perfectly normal human being who could maintain a coherent, even relatively amusing, conversation, but the other half I was like a malfunctioning robot who lacked any social grace and spouted random information and non sequiturs at a pace that would make the Road Runner jealous. The worst part was, I never knew which it was going to be. At least today, I had Jill and Kayla for backup.

I watched him come closer. It wasn't fair, even his walk was sexy. How was I supposed to stay cool and calm around someone like him?

Kayla nudged me.

"Hey, Wes," I squeaked.

He turned and gave me a smile. Did I mention he had the best smile? It took over his whole face and totally lit up his eyes. And that dimple . . . there was a good chance I was going to pass out. But I had to keep talking. I knew that. "How was your vacation?" I asked.

"It was great."

Great. *Great?* Great is not how you describe a breakup. Maybe he and Leora really were still together, and he just took down the pictures to protect her privacy from prying eyes like mine.

"How was yours?" he asked.

"It was good." I didn't want to talk about me. I wanted to know what was happening with *him*. I needed answers.

"Missed you at the bus stop today." Wait. Did I really say that? Would he think I was into him? That wasn't good. Unless he was into me, too. But he probably wasn't. "I mean, everyone was wondering where you were," I said, covering just to be safe.

His smile got bigger, if that was even possible, and he held up a set of keys. "That's because I drove in."

"You got a car?" I practically screamed.

I hoped he took it as excitement, but the fact was, I was freaking out. If he drove to school, that meant I lost valuable morning time with him. He was pretty much the only reason I didn't hit snooze on my alarm clock and managed to get myself to the bus stop on time.

"Yep," he said. "My grandmother decided it was time to stop driving, and she gave me her car. My family and I just drove it back from Florida."

I didn't know what to say. My head was spinning. "Cool" was all I could sputter out.

Jill elbowed me to keep going. Only, words weren't coming. I racked my brain. It was still empty. I didn't want the conversation to just end, so I said the first thing that popped into my mind. "Leora."

The are-you-serious, shocked look on Jill's face told me I had said the wrong thing. Why was I blurting out the name of Wes's maybe-hopefully-ex-girlfriend? I needed to fix this. "It'll make things easier for you to see her now," I stammered. "Leora, that is. You know, having a car and all." Just fabulous, I was having one of my word meltdowns. At least this one wasn't too bad, and he'd mentioned his girlfriend to me in the past, so it wasn't *that* awkward for me to bring her up. I hoped not anyway.

"We actually broke up."

Yes! Do not shriek with joy. Do not shriek with joy. Be sensitive. Be likable. "I'm sorry."

"Thanks," Wes answered, and put his history book in his backpack.

That was it?!! No explanation? No story? I wanted details.

"What happened?" Kayla asked.

Go, Kayla! Coming through for me again. And herself. She knew not knowing who dumped whom meant hours' worth of conversation with me speculating.

"It just wasn't working out," he said. "And she's a senior and got accepted early decision to Stanford. It just kind of made sense."

I nodded in agreement. Not just because I wanted him, but because they clearly didn't belong together. Love didn't need to make sense. It was supposed to be a passionate, blinding, can't-live-without-you, all-encompassing type of thing, at least that's what I hoped. It wasn't as if I had actually experienced it myself. Not truly. I mean, did it count as love if I never told Wes how I felt, and he didn't feel it back?

All I knew was that if he were my boyfriend and he wound up moving to California, it wouldn't change how I felt about him. I'd try to make it work. Things worth having aren't always meant to come easy. That's how I justified my mild obsession with him anyway.

An awkward silence fell over us. "Now that you have a car, I bet people are already hitting you up for rides," Jill said, breaking the tension.

"My parents and I are still in negotiations over the rules." He leaned his head back against the locker. "They think the car should just be for me to drive myself to and from school, lacrosse practice, and things like that, and that I shouldn't have anyone along for the ride to distract me."

They were probably also worried that people would take advantage. Wes was awesome, but he wasn't very good at saying no, which is how he wound up tutoring three people in geometry, cochairing the school recycling program, and getting roped into just about every event and activity his friends were a part of. It was a lot for one person, but somehow he managed to pull it off. It was impressive actually.

Even though it was probably for Wes's own good, I still wished his parents had waited to take a stand. It crushed any hope I had of his offering to take me to school. "That sucks," I said.

"Yeah, it does. But I'm working on them, and I have a feeling I'll win." He tossed his bag over his shoulder and winked at me. "Then you won't have to worry about waiting for the bus in the morning, either." Then he nodded at all of us and walked away.

I felt superglued to the ground. When I was confident he was out of earshot, I turned to Jill and Kayla and gave a silent scream. "Did that just happen?"

"Yes," Jill said, and all three of us started jumping as inconspicuously as possible.

Wes winked at me! And basically said he wanted to drive me to school. Although he could have just been acting neighborly, but if he wasn't . . . there was a chance. A chance that Wes Rosenthal actually liked me!

2

I was pretty much floating by the time last period approached. My imagination had warped into superdrive thinking of all the amazing ways my romance with Wes could unfold. I pictured him confessing his undying love the first time he drove me to school, telling me he had always thought I was the one for him but was nervous I might not feel the same way. Then proclaiming that he decided to take the chance because the idea of living without me as his girlfriend for even one moment longer was too much to take. And that was just one of the tamer scenarios. Sure, I knew I was going over the top, but I didn't care. I had hope!

"I'm glad I caught you." Jill rushed into my geometry class as I was packing up my stuff. "There's something you should know."

Her tone was enough to allow dread to cloud my cheerful mood. "What?"

Most people had already cleared out of the room, but Jill lowered her voice just the same. "Amanda and Cody broke up today. Right after lunch."

"So?" I said. Amanda Andrews was not exactly my favorite

person. She was one of those people who always acted superior and tried to make everyone else feel like pond scum.

"Well," Jill said, looking at the floor. "Rumor has it she did it because of Wes. She heard he was single and decided to go after him."

I walked out of the classroom, and Jill followed. I felt numb. Whatever Amanda wanted, Amanda got. It was always that way. And if she wanted Wes . . .

"I'm sorry," Jill said. "I just wanted you to know. But it doesn't mean he's going to want her. You are so much better in every way."

I appreciated her saying that, but it wasn't true. Amanda was stunning. Like just-walked-off-the-set-of-a-CW-drama stunning. Half black, half Korean, with high cheekbones, hair down to her belly button, perfect skin, and confidence that oozed out of every pore. How was I supposed to compete with that?

The warning bell rang. "Em, I'm serious," Jill said. "You're amazing. If Wes is smart, which you've told me a million times that he is, he knows that." Then she ran off to class, and I continued on to English.

Maybe she was right. And he did seem flirty this morning. I was probably working myself up over nothing.

Or maybe I wasn't. As I turned the corner for class, there she was—Amanda Andrews, standing outside the door to Mrs. Heller's class—and she wasn't alone. She was with Wes. *My* Wes, and her hand was on his arm. "I better get going," she said.

"See you later," he answered, and winked at her.

He might as well have flung a dart in my eye.

10

The final bell rang, and Amanda pushed past me. "Watch it," she said, shooting me a glare. I didn't have the energy to respond.

I somehow found myself in the back of the room, seated at my desk, but I wasn't quite sure how I got there. Everything seemed foggy. Did the wink he gave me earlier mean nothing? Did I only see what I wanted to see? Or was I just too late, had Amanda already made her move? *Wes didn't like me*. The wink didn't mean anything.

"Hey," Wes said, turning to me. He was seated directly to my right. "I hear Heller is going to announce—"

He was cut off by Kirsten, a cute soccer player, who turned around in her seat to face him. "I saw you drive up today. Nice car, Rosenthal. You'll have to give me a ride sometime."

He winked at her, and she turned back around, almost crowing.

Seriously? Had Wes become a serial winker over winter break? Was there something wrong with his eye that gave him some sort of a tic? I couldn't take it. "What's with all the winking?" I blurted out. I hadn't meant to say that aloud.

"What?" he asked.

He looked a little taken aback. "Nothing, just trying to be funny," I answered, and threw in some lame ha-ha-has to get the point across. Boy, was I striking out. "What were you saying before? What is Heller announcing?"

"She's—"

He was cut off again. This time by Mrs. Heller herself.

"I know many of you have been waiting for this, and it's time!" she said. "We're taking sign-ups for Shakespeare in the Heights Night!" Most of the class seemed excited, which I didn't quite understand. It was just an evening of Shakespearean scenes that the school put on every year. For some reason, it's kind of a big deal in town. Awards even get handed out for best actor, costume, set design, direction, and so on. Shaker Heights High School's own little Tony Awards. But if you asked me, it was totally boring. I opted out last year. "And as added incentive for your participation," Mrs. Heller continued, "I will drop your lowest quiz score."

That definitely raised the stakes. I raised my hand. "What exactly does participation include?" As much as I hated Shakespeare, I had to take part.

"Behind-the-scenes work, acting—"

"Showing up to watch?" Cody Burns butted in.

"Okay," Mrs. Heller said. "I'll give you something for that. I'll give you an extra ten points on your lowest quiz."

"Sweet," he said.

Maybe it was for him, but for me, ten points wasn't going to do anything. I got a solid fifteen on my last quiz; turning that into a twenty-five still equaled an F. I needed that score dropped; it was killing my grade.

Mrs. Heller gave us more information about the show and passed out flyers detailing how we could get involved.

"Are you going to do it this year?" Wes asked.

I played with the edges of the sheet. "I have no choice." Although I had no idea what I was going to do. Backstage seemed tedious, but performing wasn't really an option. I still had nightmares from second grade, the last time I was on stage. I was a horse in some silly, little Old MacDonald play. All I had to do was say "neigh" and walk seven steps to the left, but I panicked and ran to get away. I wound up knocking over half the scenery with my gigantic costume, then to top it off, I fell off the stage and broke my wrist. I have shied away from performing ever since. But like it or not, I had to be involved in the production somehow.

"I kinda figured as much," he said. "I saw your last quiz."

"Yeah, it wasn't pretty." (I swore I was never going to put off my reading to watch another Kardashian marathon again. Although, to be fair, it was for a very good reason. My cousin didn't make her school's varsity basketball team and was majorly bummed. She lived too far away to go visit, so, to cheer her up, I called her, and we stayed on the phone all night, turning on our respective TVs and dissecting and commenting on each episode. It got kind of addicting—and it made her seem to forget what happened. Family first, right? That should count for something.) "What about you?"

His eyes glanced over the choices listed on the paper. "I think I'll try out for one of the scenes and see what happens."

"Cool," I said. "Which one?"

"Romeo and Juliet."

Romeo and Juliet?! Was he serious? That was supposed to be the most romantic play ever. I couldn't let this opportunity pass. I could be his Juliet. I quickly weighed the pros and the cons in my head. The pros were awesome. They were, basically, Wes. But the cons were, well, too huge to ignore. Still . . .

Don't do it, Emily. Don't do it, Emily. Don't do it, Emily. But there was no stopping me. "Nice. That's what I was planning on trying for, too." And just like that, with a few simple words, I found myself in way over my head.

3

"Don't forget to breathe when you get up on stage," Kayla said as we stood outside the auditorium. "I'll be there the whole time. You got this."

I nodded, but I wasn't so sure. Was I seriously trying out for *Romeo and Juliet*?

A few classmates waved and wished me luck as they passed us and went inside. I managed to squeak out a "you too," but the longer I stood there, the more nervous I got.

Why did it have to be an open audition? I didn't need everyone watching me. I mean, I knew that would happen if I got the part, but that would be after tons of rehearsals. Mrs. Heller gave us only a week to prepare for the audition. "I don't know if I can do this, Kayla."

"Yes, you can. You've been practicing. You sound good. And Jill signed up to direct the *Romeo and Juliet* scene. How much more perfect can it get? She can cast you and Wes. What better way to fall in love than portraying one of the most romantic couples of all time?"

"What if I'm awful?"

"You're not. I heard you practice. And besides, Jill is an

amazing director. You know how important this is to her. She'll make you look good. She'll work you to the bone until you are the best Juliet that ever lived."

That was true. I could count on Jill. She'd guarantee I was ready. "You're right, I'm just having second-grade flashbacks."

"Well, in that performance, you wore a *horse* costume. I'd have nightmares, too. This time you will be wearing an ah-mazing gown designed by yours truly. Trust me, you will want this dress on your body."

Kayla was a superskilled designer. Most of what she wore, she made herself, and she always looked incredible. I knew whatever she came up with for the scene would be breath-taking. "Okay, you win. Let's do this."

She gave a little clap and swung open the auditorium door for us. A lot more people were there than I anticipated. All the directors from all the scenes were already seated. They would be judging us. But a big chunk of my classmates were in the room, too. I had signed up for the first slot, thinking every-one would get there later. I guess everyone wanted to size up the competition.

"Don't let all the people get to you. Your only problem is going to be that all the directors are going to want you," Kayla said.

She was a good friend. One who was totally stretching the truth, but I appreciated it just the same. "I highly doubt that."

"Seriously, though, what happens if someone else wants to cast you?"

I had taken precautions. On the audition slip, we got to fill out our top three choices and check off if we'd accept any role.

I didn't. "I said I'd only take Juliet." There was no way I was going on stage if Wes wasn't there.

"And what if Wes doesn't get Romeo?"

I wasn't worried about that. "It's the part he wants, and look at him, is there anyone in this school who is more leading-man material?"

"You have a point there," she said.

We took a seat near the back, and I kept going over my script. All the aspiring Juliets were told to do a short piece from act 2, scene 5, where Juliet's waiting for her nurse to come back. She had sent her to meet Romeo with a message. It wasn't the worst piece of Shakespeare I had seen, but it still wasn't great. I really hated this stuff, but it was worth pushing that aside. This was for love.

As I went over the lines for the umpteenth time, an uber-perky laugh filled the room. "I'm so glad you decided to do this with me."

It was Amanda, and she was walking down the aisle with *my* crush.

"We're going to make the perfect Romeo and Juliet, don't you think?" she asked.

WHAT? Was that why Wes was trying out for Romeo? So he could star opposite . . . *her*?!! Amanda had talked to him before Mrs. Heller made the announcement to our class. She would have already known about the scene night because she had English earlier. Here I was hoping I could be Wes's Juliet, when the whole time he was doing this for Amanda? I didn't know what to think or what to do.

My thoughts must have gotten away from me, because the

next thing I knew Kayla was nudging me. "They're calling your name."

Part of me didn't want to try out anymore, but I knew that wasn't the answer. Amanda hadn't won yet, and I couldn't let her. This was my chance for Wes to see me in a new light: as his love interest. I needed this part, so regardless of how I felt, I had to act confident. That was half the battle. So I stood up, and with my head held high, I practically strutted to the stage. This role was mine for the taking, and I wasn't about to blow it.

4

"Start whenever you're ready," Jill called out. All the directors were sitting in the fourth row. As I stood on stage, I scanned the room. Seeing people staring back at me was more than a little daunting.

My stomach turned, and I flashed back to the summer. My friends somehow persuaded me to ride the second-tallest roller coaster in the world. I was petrified. The drop was 420 feet, and I screamed all the way down. Afterward, I threw up. Twice. And yet, right now, looking out at all the eyes on me, that roller coaster seemed like a carousel.

"Ticktock," Ryan Watkins, who was directing one of the other scenes, said while tapping his wrist. "When she said, 'whenever you're ready,' she didn't really mean *whenever*. She meant *go*."

I knew I had to do something. Either start the monologue or leave. I had been up there lightly swaying for what seemed like forever. I wanted to turn and run. I wanted to say never mind. But then I caught Wes's eye, and he smiled at me.

And that smile melted my fears. Okay, maybe not every one of them, but enough to get me to start delivering my lines.

Enough to make me realize I could do this. Enough to make me realize how very badly I wanted this to work out. "The clock struck nine when I did send the nurse; in half an hour she promised to return. Perchance she cannot meet him: that's not so. O, she is lame!"

I glanced back at him, and he was still focused on me, his eyes encouraging, as if he knew I could do it. I had seen that look before—many years ago. I had fallen off my bike and skinned my legs and arms and refused to ever ride again. But the next day, Wes came over and said I should try again, that he'd go with me. Even though I was terrified, I said okay. He waited for me at the end of the driveway and cheered me on as I made my way toward him. He had the same look then as he was giving me now. It said, *You can do this.* I smiled back at him as I recited, "Love's heralds should be thoughts, which ten times faster glide than the sun's beams." I didn't quite know what the line meant, but saying the word *love* while looking at Wes was enough to make me feel as if I could do anything.

When I finished, Jill gave me a thumbs-up, and I headed back to my seat. Wes winked at me as I passed him, and despite his new role as the winking bandit of Ohio, it still made me feel good. He was my Romeo. Now I just needed us both to land the parts.

"That was great," Kayla said as I took my seat.

"You really think so?"

"Yes, this is so your role. I can't wait to design the dress for you!"

I felt so relieved. I had done it. And I hadn't fallen off the stage or broken a wrist or knocked anything over. I was actually okay.

Although I hated Shakespeare, I stuck around for the rest of the auditions. I liked having Wes there encouraging me, and I thought maybe some of my classmates could use a friendly face, too. And I was a very good audience member. I smiled and nodded at everyone on stage in case they needed some support—even my competition. And I applauded. For everyone. Even though I was almost the only one doing it.

My ears perked up when Wes's name was called. He totally owned the stage. You couldn't help but watch his every move. The way he maneuvered his body so regally, the easy way he smiled when he spoke about Juliet, the way his arm flexed when he pointed to the balcony where his love was supposed to be. Sure, I had no idea what he was saying, but that was Shakespeare's fault—not his. Wes still managed to make the words sound sexy. Shakespeare owed him one.

"You are definitely the best Juliet," Kayla said.

"Thanks," I said, but unfortunately there was still one more to go. Amanda Andrews had signed up for the final audition slot.

She virtually glided onto the stage when they called her name. Then in a grandiose motion, she threw her script to the floor and began to speak. And she was good. *Really good*. Like made-me-almost-understand-what-the-whole-monologue-was-about good. I felt the urgency and desperation in her voice. Her need for the nurse to come back so she'd know if Romeo got her message and what his response was. She looked like a girl madly in love. Amanda Andrews could act.

Everyone applauded when she finished. Really applauded, not just the polite smattering some auditioners got. These were legit.

"Now that is how you do it," Ryan said.

Amanda crushed my plan. There was no way I was getting to play Juliet now.

Everyone was singing her praises. Not that I could blame the crowd. Apparently, she had stolen the show last year, too, with her scene from *The Tempest*. My only chance to get cast was if Ryan or another director fought to have her in their scene. They had to want her. How could they not? But still . . . if she wanted my part, she'd have it.

As if that wasn't bad enough, when Amanda left the stage and came down the aisle, Wes was nodding, smiling, and looking at her like she was . . . well . . . his Juliet.

I was in trouble.

5

Jill sent me a text. **Meet me in the bathroom.**

She was already waiting there when I showed up. "Em . . ."

I shook my head. She didn't need to say anything. I could tell by her face. I wasn't going to be Juliet. "You don't need to explain. I was there. I get it. You have to cast Amanda."

"I'm—"

I cut her off. "It's okay. She deserves it. And I know how important this is to you. You have a better shot at best director with her anyway."

Her face looked pained. "I'd still pick you if I could, but she said she'd only accept the part of Juliet, and it's not just my decision." Jill wrapped her arms around herself. "I'm sorry. I know how much you wanted this. And Wes . . ."

"Stop," I said. "It's not your fault. I get it." It sucked, and of course I was upset that I wasn't going to get to work with Wes, but I understood. And I certainly wasn't going to blame Jill for doing what she had to do.

"I just wanted you to hear it from me."

I leaned back against the counter. "Thanks."

"I'm really sorry, Em. If it makes you feel better, even

though I know Amanda is really talented, I'm not looking forward to working with her. Did you see what she did when she passed in her audition sheet? She *patted* me on the head and said, 'You're the lucky little director who gets to work with me.'"

Jill must have been fuming. She hated when people commented on her height. She said there was a lot more to her than her size (which there was) and got majorly annoyed when people referred to her four-foot-ten stature. Amanda knew this. Jill told her off after Amanda made fun of her last year. Clearly, the message didn't sink in. Patting her on the head? That was so patronizing.

"She's horrible," I said. "I can't stand her." I got along with just about everybody at school, yet there was something about Amanda (probably the way she treated everyone) that made me want to scream.

"It gets worse," Jill said. "She stipulated that she'd only take Wes as her Romeo. It's driving me crazy. Who does she think she is? She's not in charge of casting. She is going to be such a pain to work with. Sapna directed her in *The Tempest* last year, and this year she won't even work on the production. Her experience was totally soured. Sapna said she had had enough of the self-entitled, know-it-all Amanda actor–types to fill a lifetime."

I wish I could say I was surprised, but I'd heard Amanda try to control, manipulate, and bully one too many people to think she'd be any other way. "You're a great director, though," I assured Jill. "I know you'll make it work."

"I still wish you were a part of the scene, though. I loved the idea of helping bring you and Wes together. Maybe you can be my assistant or something?"

Being at rehearsals could help, but it wasn't the same as being thought of as Wes's love interest—even if it was just in a play. Then it hit me. "Jill, that's it! You're a genius."

"Huh? Because I want to make you my assistant?"

"No, I'm thinking more of the *or something*. You can make me Amanda's understudy!"

"What? Are you nuts? One-night school performances don't have understudies. Aren't you the one who keeps reminding me this isn't Broadway?"

"Well, maybe that should change."

"Em, no one's going to want to learn all those lines to never get to say them."

"Then don't make *everyone* do it. Just make me," I said.

"So the only person in the whole production who will have an understudy is Amanda?" Jill asked. "She's going to love that one."

"Who cares? She thinks she has all the control. Let's turn it around. Blame it on me. Tell her, tell the directors, tell everyone I really need the extra credit, and there's no other place for me. That they should see me trying to build a set or hang lights. That this will cause the least damage to the production as a whole. They'll understand. They've all seen how klutzy I am. They'll think you're even taking one for the team. Besides, they know we're friends. They won't care. You can even tell Mrs. Heller that my role is understudy/director's assistant. And I will assist you—in whatever you need. I promise."

"I don't know if it will work," Jill said, but she looked as if she was seriously considering my proposal. I just needed one final push.

"And come on, it's extra backup for you. If Amanda gets all

24

dramatic and quits, you still have a Juliet. And I'm practically Amanda's size. I'll even fit into the costume. This is a win-win. Make me the understudy, please?" I folded my hands together and got down on my knees. "Please, please, please, please, please, please."

"All right, all right," she said. "Get up. I'll do it."

I jumped to my feet and pulled her into a big bear hug. "You are the best friend ever. Thank you so much. You won't regret this."

I could tell she thought this plan was out there, but I knew it would work! It was the perfect scenario and so much better than being the real Juliet. I was going to be able to sit in on every rehearsal, get close to Romeo, and never have to take the stage. My plan to win over Wes was officially under way!

6

I skipped—literally skipped—into the first R&J rehearsal. Amanda and Wes were already on stage. Jill was there, too. I waved. Jill and Wes waved back. Amanda glowered. To say she was not excited to have an understudy was putting it mildly. Jill told me she had spent two hours on the phone calming her down. And while I felt bad that Jill had to go through that, I was kind of loving that my-way-or-no-way Amanda was being knocked off her pedestal.

I took a seat in the middle of the auditorium and got comfortable. Being an understudy was the life. The actors had to do all the work, while I got to relax. Part of me wanted to just put on my iPod and chill, but I owed it to Jill to at the very least learn my lines. And how hard could it be? I had every day in rehearsal to do it. I pulled out the pages Jill had photocopied for me. There were only four, but, man, was there a lot of words. This was going to be a little more challenging than I thought.

My eyes started to glaze over as I read through Juliet's lines. What was I looking at? Sentences like, "How cam'st thou hither, tell me, and wherefore?," "Yet, if thou swear'st, thou mayst prove

false," and "Therefore thou mayst think my 'havior light."
This was insane. Why did everyone love this play so much? It
made no sense.

For the next thirty minutes I tried to hammer the words
into my brain, but nothing stuck. But it was only the first day;
by showtime I'd be fine.

"Okay," Jill said, "Wes, you can take a seat. Amanda, let's
work on your monologue for a bit." She turned back to me and
smiled. She really was amazing; she was giving me Wes time!
Although Amanda's monologue was no joke. It was a gazillion
lines long and was full of what had to be random words arbi-
trarily put together.

"Want to run lines?" Wes asked, taking a seat next to me.

Could hearts stop when confronted with too much hotness?
Because I felt like mine was about to. "With me?"

"Yeah, with you. You're the understudy, aren't you?" He
winked at me. And, okay, I'll admit, his new little habit was
growing on me—even if he did share it with way too many
people.

"Let's start with your line," he said.

I nodded, although I didn't know how I was going to talk.
He was sitting so close, and he smelled really good, like a mix
of shampoo and outdoors and boy—a really handsome boy. "Ay
me!" I read.

"She speaks: O, speak again, bright angel! for thou art as
glorious to this night, being o'er my head as is a winged mes-
senger of heaven unto the white-upturned wondr'ing eyes of
mortals that fall back to gaze on him when he bestrides the
lazy-pacing clouds, and sails upon the bosom of the air."

Ninety percent of that made no sense to me, but I did

manage to catch that he called me, or rather Juliet, an angel and glorious, and the rest didn't matter. That was all I needed.

"It's your line," he said.

Right. *Focus, Emily.* You're supposed to be rehearsing, not staring longingly into Wes's eyes. But they were such nice eyes. So dark and intense. It was hard to focus. "Sorry," I said.

"Don't be," he said. "This stuff is hard. I'm kinda wondering what I got myself into."

"I don't even know what most of these lines mean," I confessed.

"That's okay. I didn't, either. I spent three hours online last night trying to translate them into something I could make sense of. Like, did you know *wherefore* means 'why,' not 'where'?"

"Really? Why—or I guess, wherefore—couldn't Shakespeare just write *why*? It would be so much easier."

"Seriously. But you'll get it." He put his hand on my shoulder. And I was pretty sure I was about to melt into a puddle on the ground. "Want to keep going?"

I nodded.

Only, someone else had another idea. "Wes," Amanda said, marching over to us, "I'm having a little bit of a hard time with my monologue. I think it would help if you were up there with me, and I could direct it to you. Would that be okay?"

He hesitated before standing up. "Yeah, sure."

It might have just been my imagination, but it kind of seemed as if he didn't want to go up there.

"And, Emily," Amanda said, "be a doll and give me a hand. I need to make about a dozen signs for the dance. If you can go to the art room for me and bang that out, I'd appreciate it. And make them nice. We want people to actually come to the event."

"I'm your understudy, not your gopher," I told her.

"Wellllll," she said, "when I spoke to Jill last night, she did say the reason for the understudy was because the Juliet part was so demanding. I thought that meant you'd help lighten my workload. I wouldn't want to miss rehearsals to get it all done. Then Jill may not get the winning scene she was hoping for."

Amanda was evil. I wanted to call her bluff. There was no way Miss Theater-Is-My-Life would risk not giving a perfect performance. But she could make things extrahard for Jill during rehearsals, and I didn't want to be the reason for that. I looked over at my best friend, who was biting two nails at once. I had to fix this before she gnawed them all off. "Fine, whatever."

"Thank you," Jill mouthed, and I nodded.

"Great," Amanda said. "There's already one sign made. Just make the others like it. And when you're done, if you wouldn't mind hanging them up. Oh, and make a flyer, too, while you're at it."

"Okay." Jill walked over to us. "Let's get moving. Another director takes over the room in an hour and a half, and we have a lot to do."

"I'll see you later, Em," Wes said. "Need a ride home?"

What?!! Was he really asking me? I was almost too stunned to answer. "I . . . I . . . thought you couldn't . . ."

"Yes," Jill interrupted my stuttering, "she would love one. She'll meet you outside after rehearsal. Now let's get going." She put one hand on Amanda's back and the other on Wes's and guided them back to the stage.

Jill was actually touching Wes Rosenthal. I wondered what his back felt like. A wall, maybe a little softer than that, but still totally toned. She would have to give me a detailed report later. And I was going to have stories of my own! Thanks to Jill, I had accepted a ride home with Romeo.

7

Wes was leaning against his car when I went outside. He looked like a hot model in a car advertisement.

"Sorry I'm late," I said, trying not to sound too out of breath. I had raced around the school to hang up the posters as fast as I could so I could meet Wes on time. But Amanda's arts-and-crafts project had taken a lot longer than I'd anticipated.

"You're fine," he said. "How was poster duty?" He hadn't moved to get into the car, so I wasn't sure if I should just get into the passenger side or stand in front of him and talk a bit.

"Not too bad," I said, staying put. I figured the longer we were outside, the longer I got to spend with him. "A little more glitter than I imagined."

"I can see that." Then he reached toward my face. "Close your eyes."

Oh. My. God. What was happening?! Was he going to kiss me?! I did as instructed, and then I felt his hand lightly dust my cheek. There was a good chance I was going to spontaneously combust. But if I had to go, this was definitely the way to do it.

"Got it," he said, and I opened my eyes to look. On his finger were a few pieces of glitter. "They were right near your eye."

"Thanks," I said. I wasn't sure how I was still able to talk. It might not have been a kiss, but it was still Wes touching me. On purpose. My heart was beating faster than one of those crazy tech songs they always played on Friday nights at The Heights—the really cheesy, but still sort of fun, entertainment/ student center. I hoped he couldn't hear it. "If you're afraid about me getting glitter in your car, it's okay, I mean, I'd get it, I wouldn't want that all over my car." Oh no. The babbling was starting. *Calm down, Emily*, I instructed myself, but it wasn't working. "I can have my mom come get me, or my dad, depending on who's home. Or there's a good chance Jill's probably still here going over notes and things. She's very good with details. I can go look. Maybe I should."

"It's not a problem. Honest." He walked over to the passenger side of the car and opened the door. "Please," he said, and gestured inside. "You're my first nonfamily passenger."

I got in, and he shut the door. I really wasn't kidding about the combusting. I just hoped it wouldn't be too hard for him to clean up afterward. I wouldn't want to ruin his new car. "Are you sure it's okay?" I asked once he was in the driver's seat. "I thought your parents didn't want you to drive anyone."

"We're reaching an agreement," he said. "They're going to try to back off unless I give them a reason not to. They still don't want me to become the Shaker Heights chauffeur or anything, but a ride home for a friend is fine." I'd rather he had used the term *love interest*, or *gorgeous understudy*, or *future girlfriend*, than just *friend*, but I'd take it. "Besides," he said, "you live down the street from me. It doesn't make sense to make your parents come all the way down here when I pass your house anyway."

"Thanks."

"Any time," he answered. And he could be sure I planned to take advantage of that offer.

My nerves were slowly subsiding. He seemed so relaxed and at ease, it was almost calming. "I'm very jealous you have your own car," I said. My family had only one since my dad primarily worked from home, and my parents didn't think a second vehicle was necessary. "I'm trying to save up enough to get one, too."

"I was kind of surprised my parents let me have it," Wes said. "But with Neal's crazy schedule, it helps them not to have to worry about picking me up and dropping me off places." Neal was Wes's brother. I didn't know him very well, but Wes talked about him a lot, and I'd seen a ton of pictures on GroupIt and things. Neal was two years below us in school, but he was younger than most freshmen. He was some sort of math genius and skipped two grades. He even took a college engineering course in the morning, before he headed to Shaker Heights High. He was that crazy smart, and Wes was superprotective of him.

"Is he doing any better?"

Wes shrugged. "He says he's fine, but I don't know. He never hangs out with anyone. It's either school, homework, lectures at the college, or hanging out with the family. He doesn't seem to have any friends. I'm worried he's not fitting in."

The concern was warranted. It must have been hard for Neal. Most of the high schoolers had to see him as a lot younger. He had a baby face and was really short. But then again, that was also Wes when he was thirteen. "It's a hard age, regardless. Must be extrahard for him. I wouldn't go back."

A huge smile spread over his face again. "What would you know about going through a hard age?" Wes said. "You skipped right over the awkward stage."

"Did not, and look who's talking."

"Me?!" he asked. "Do you not remember the gargantuan teeth and forehead that were way too big for my face? I was also the smallest kid in class, and people thought I was lying about my age I looked so young."

I couldn't help but laugh. All of that was definitely true, but despite it all—or maybe because of it—I still thought he was the best-looking guy in school, even then. Sure, now he was more than a foot taller, his features perfectly fit his face, his teeth looked human-size, and everyone could pretty much universally agree that he was handsome, but my crush on Wes went back as far as I could remember.

"See," he said, laughing with me. "It was bad."

"No, it wasn't. It was cute."

"You were the lucky one. I don't even think you ever got a zit," he said.

"That's not true," I objected. And then I realized something—this conversation meant Wes thought about me over the years—and thought I looked good. Clearly, he wasn't superobservant, since I had more than my fair share of pimples and random awkwardness, but he didn't see any of that. "There was a giant one on my forehead that caused me to get those monster bangs. They were uncontrollable. They wouldn't lay flat; they wouldn't curl away. They shot out in multidirections. It took me, like, a can of hairspray a day to get them to do what I wanted, and even then a cowlick would pop up."

"That's nothing," he argued. "Adorable even. You had it easy."

"Okay, now I know you're just saying that to try to prove your point. Those bangs still give me nightmares. But you don't think that was bad? How about this? One of my boobs grew faster than the other, and I had to shove tissues into one side of my bra. And they'd sometimes fall out in gym class." *No, no, no, no.* Did I just say that to *Wes*? Was I really talking about my boobs? And stuffing bras? I so needed a chaperone at all times to save me from myself. "They're even now," I added, so there wasn't any confusion. "My boobs, I mean. No more tissues." I really needed to stop talking.

But then he just laughed, and it all seemed okay. "You win," he said, "maybe you didn't have it all easy. The gym class must have been kind of horrifying for you."

It had been. Fortunately, it was all girls, but that didn't mean they let it go. Amanda was the first to seize on my embarrassment, and for about a year instead of Emily Stein, she called me Emily Stuffs-My-Bra. I was surprised Wes hadn't heard about it—or more likely he had and was just being polite. "But I survived it. I'm okay, and I know your brother will be, too. I had Kayla and Jill, but Neal has you. He's lucky."

"Thanks," he said right as we pulled up to my house. "Here we are."

"I appreciate the ride."

Wes tipped his head in my direction. "See you tomorrow, Juliet."

"I'm just an imposter," I reminded him.

"Well, then good night whatever your name is."

I smiled at him as I got out of the car. "Good night, Romeo."

Maybe Shakespeare wasn't so bad after all.

8

"I cannot believe you accepted an early morning shift," my friend and Northside Grocery partner-in-crime Dhonielle Jackson said as we stacked cans of peas and corn niblets.

"You and me both." I had been working at the store for about a year now, primarily weekends, vacations, and an occasional shift during the week, but I always went for the late-afternoon or evening hours. Mornings are not my thing. At all. "I didn't have a choice if I wanted to work this weekend. Amanda insisted we rehearse yesterday and today because she wanted to have dance committee meetings on Thursday and Friday. So to do everything, I had to come in now."

"That's rough."

"Tell me about it," I said, trying to suppress a yawn.

Dhonielle slid over another box filled with canned goods, and we both started unpacking. "You could have gotten out of work."

"Yeah, but that wouldn't put me any closer to a car. You know the only way my parents will even think of letting me get one is if I come up with the money on my own and 'show how responsible I am,'" I said, putting on my best Dad voice.

"Couldn't you skip rehearsal? You could survive a couple of days without Wes," she teased.

I swatted her arm. "It's not *only* about Wes. I couldn't do that to Jill. I need to be there. I'm struggling to learn these lines. I don't know how you do it."

Dhonielle was in the *A Midsummer Night's Dream* scene and loved to perform. Especially comedy. She had even formed an improv troupe at our school. "You're just overthinking it," she said. "If you can ace chemistry and geometry the way you do, you should be able to handle Shakespeare."

"They are totally different," I argued. "Math and science have rules and formulas. They are things I will actually use. I am never going to need Shakespeare. I want to do engineering, coding, things like that. I can't imagine the requirements will include my knowing some ridiculous sonnet. Shakespeare makes up his own words. What is that?" I pulled the script from my pocket. I had been carrying it with me everywhere, trying to study whenever I got a free moment. "Listen to this stuff, 'Fain would I dwell on form, fain, fain deny.' I mean, come on."

"You know those are real words, right?"

"Yes, I know they are words. But no sane person would ever put them together. It would be like my saying, " 'Sorry, Dhonielle, you have to stack-eth the rest-eth of these cans, because I fain, fain deny.' That's just dumb."

"Well, you are using the words totally out of context."

I threw my script at her. "You know what I mean."

"Do you want help with it? I can run lines with you."

"Really?"

She nodded.

"Yes!" I said, and pulled her into a hug. Maybe this day at

work wouldn't be so bad after all. "I so need your help. You know Amanda keeps giving me all those stupid things to do so I can't practice during rehearsals. I seriously think she may be part evil."

"You have to do your Amanda impression again," she pleaded. Dhonielle was also in the I-hate-Amanda camp. The two were friends when we were younger, but then Dhonielle got the lead in the school musical, and Amanda got annoyed and turned their whole group against her.

"No, I can't. People are starting to show up to grocery shop."

"Then do it quickly. Come on," she begged. "It's hysterical."

"It's a little mean," I objected.

"No, what she does to you and Jill is mean. This is satire. It's totally acceptable."

I *did* need to blow off some Amanda steam. After more than a month of Little Miss Shakespeare's divalike behavior, I was truly ready to scream. Not only was I stuck waking up at an unearthly hour because of her, but she was constantly insulting me at rehearsals. A little *satire* seemed warranted. "Fine, last time," I relented, and started pumping my fists and stamping my feet on the ground. "I want to do it my way. Jiillllllllllllllll, you need to get Emily out of here. I can't concentrate when she's watching me. She has crazy eyes. And she breathes soooo loud." I did my best Darth Vader impression. "How can anyone think when she's near them? She really should come with a warning sign. And I don't like the way Wes talks to her. He should only pay attention to meeee!" Then I got down on the ground and started kicking my feet like a two-year-old having a tantrum. I will admit, that last part was an embellishment, but Amanda really did say that stuff about my eyes and breathing. Yes, even the Darth Vader part. Which is totally not true, FYI.

"Emily, are you okay?"

I looked up. Mr. Martinez was looking down at me. He was one of our regulars, a supernice man in his seventies. I jumped up and saw Dhonielle trying to contain her laughter. I was totally going to kill her. "Yes, I'm fine." I wondered if my face was bright red. "I was just, ummm, showing Dhonielle, uhhh, something . . ."

"Yeah," Dhonielle piped in. "Something she's working on for school. She wants my improv group to expand to sketch comedy. She wrote that last bit herself."

"Oh," Mr. Martinez said, "it was very convincing. Keep up the good work."

I felt so stupid. "Thanks," I said as he walked away. That's what I get for making fun of Amanda. Karma kicking my butt.

I turned to Dhonielle. "If you get me fired, you are so buying me a car."

She waved her hand. "No problem, just as long as you drive me to auditions. Now let's look at these lines." She picked up my script off the ground. "Although I don't know why you are so worried. From what I just saw, you're not such a bad actress."

Sure, maybe at pretending to be Amanda, but Juliet was a whole other matter. At least no one would ever have to see me perform either one in front of an audience ever again.

9

"**W**hy are we stopping noooow?" Amanda asked, stretching the last word into a Guinness World Records–holding whine.

"Lighting needs to mark its cues," Jill answered. Her voice sounded remarkably calm for someone in the middle of a way-too-long tech/dress rehearsal. I guess, as a director, she needed to act that way, especially with someone like Amanda, who thought she was destined to be America's next big star and should be treated as such. But I was so over it.

"Well, can we pleeeease get this moving?" Amanda cried out again. "I'm not feeling well." I half expected her to stomp her feet, the way I did in the grocery store. But instead, she gave a huge grimace and clutched her side.

"Are you okay?" Jill called out as Kayla ran up to the set.

"Is the costume too tight?" Kayla asked. She had just put the finishing touches on the gown today, which was cutting it close since the performance was tomorrow.

"No." Amanda swatted her away, but she still had a look of pain.

I might have been concerned if it were anyone else, but in the last six days alone I had seen Amanda cry wolf about a dozen times. She had pretended to faint in front of Wes so he would dote on her, claimed that my voice gave her migraines and that I needed to be silent or leave the auditorium, and started weeping when she thought Jill was being too demanding and not considerate enough of a true artist's sensitive feelings.

If I were the director, I would have fired her, but Jill was a perfectionist, and even though Amanda was a nightmare to work with, she was a really good actress. And considering I was the backup choice, Amanda was Jill's best shot of winning best director, and Jill really wanted to win.

Amanda wrapped her arms around her stomach. "I'll be fine," she said.

"I can get you a ginger ale or something," Wes offered. "It might help."

"No, you need to stay and rehearse with me. Emily can go," she said, volunteering my services. "It's not like she has anything to do." Amanda hadn't let up on the idea that understudy meant personal assistant.

"Okay," I said, and headed for the vending machines. Jill gave me another silent thank-you. It was probably her eightieth since rehearsals began. She knew I was doing this for her—not Amanda. And for Wes's benefit. It would look awful if I refused to help a sick girl, even though I knew she was a total faker.

I grabbed the pop and headed back to the auditorium. At least this task took only a minute. Over the past month my Cinderella duties had escalated. Every time I said no, Amanda threatened to miss rehearsal, which freaked Jill out. So being a true best friend, I gave in. Although gradually the chores went beyond making dance posters. The past few weeks, I had the pleasure of taking Amanda's shift in the keep-our-parks-clean campaign (two hours of picking up dog doo and trash), actually ordering the decorations for the dance (she was head of the committee), and taking photos of her so she could post them on GroupIt. Basically, whenever Amanda saw me talking to Wes or trying to work on the scene (I was her understudy after all), she found me a new job.

As I stepped into the room, Wes and Amanda were walking out, and he had his arm around her, helping her stay upright. She certainly was milking this act.

"Hey," Wes said. "We decided to call it quits for tonight, so Amanda can rest. I'm gonna give her a ride home. You're okay getting to the store, right?"

I nodded. "Definitely," I said, but I was disappointed. Wes had been giving me rides after rehearsal. It was my favorite part of the day. Today he was going to drop me off for my shift at Northside Grocery. It was six minutes where I got to talk to him in an Amanda-free zone. My chance where he would maybe, hopefully, see that we were meant to be together. I handed Amanda the ginger ale. "Feel better."

Instead of thanking me for the drink, she narrowed her eyes and glared at me. "Don't get any ideas," she said, resting her head on Wes's shoulder. "I'll be back tomorrow. There's no way I'm missing this. Even if it means getting the whole school sick, I'm getting on that stage. You are not taking my place."

"Wasn't planning to," I said.

"Good," she answered, and started to walk off. Wes gave me a half smile and a small wave. There was nothing I could do but wave back as my Romeo took his Juliet and left me behind.

"Emily," Jill called out. "Can you go up on the balcony? We

want to work on the lighting. Kayla will stand in for Romeo. Okay?"

"Whatever you need."

"Thanks," she said. "You've really stepped up through all this. I know Amanda's been hard on you. I really appreciate everything. We're just going to do the blocking. We don't need the lines right now." Her expression got superintense. "But you do know them, right? Just in case?"

I gave her a thumbs-up. "Everything will be fine," I assured her. And it would be. There was no way Amanda was going to miss her star performance.

10

"Emily. Emily. Em!"

I jolted up. *Huh? What was going on? Where was I?* I looked around the room. I was still in bed, but Kayla was standing in the doorway.

"What are you doing here?" I asked, glancing at the clock. It was 10:43. Way too early to be up on a Saturday morning. Everybody, especially Kayla, knew I slept in 'til at least noon on weekends.

"You didn't answer your phone."

"Because I was *sleeping*!" I grabbed my cell. Fifteen missed calls. Four from Kayla, and eleven from Jill. "Oh my God. What happened? Is Jill okay?"

"She's fine," Kayla said.

"Then what's going on?"

"It's Amanda," she said, scrunching up her nose.

"What about her?"

"Well, you know how we all thought she was just being a drama queen yesterday, complaining about that pain in her stomach?" Kayla waited for me to nod. "Turns out it was real.

Her parents ended up taking her to the hospital. She had to have her appendix out."

"Is she okay?"

"Yeah, but she needs to stay in the hospital."

"That's awful. At least she's all right." I threw my head back down on the pillow. I felt bad for Amanda, but I wasn't quite sure why Kayla felt the need to wake me up just to tell me.

"This couldn't have waited until noon?" I asked, trying to sound as nice as I could muster. But I was so tired, and I just wanted to go back to bed. Yesterday had gone on forever—first school, then rehearsal, then a late shift at the grocery store. "Or you could have just called the landline. I have a home phone, you know. You could have left a message with my mom."

Kayla moved closer, pulled out her iPhone, and held it up to me, a sly little smile on her face. "Okay, I'll admit it, I kind of wanted to see your reaction for myself."

"To what? I mean, I'm sorry Amanda's in the hospital. But what does it have to do with me?"

"Think about it," Kayla said.

Amanda and me? The only thing we had in common was the . . .

"No, no, no, no, no, *no!*" I jumped out of bed. "This can't be happening. She can't be in the hospital! Not tonight. This is *not* happening."

But Kayla's face told me it was.

Amanda Andrews was stuck in the hospital. That meant she couldn't perform her Shakespeare scene tonight. So her understudy had to go on in her place. The understudy who volunteered only to get closer to Wes, aka Romeo Capulet . . . or

Montague . . . or whichever last name was his, and to get some extra credit. The understudy who didn't learn *any* of her lines because (a) it was really hard, (b) she was too busy doing her other schoolwork, her part-time job, and all of Amanda's chores, and (c) what was the point? UNDERSTUDIES NEVER GET TO PERFORM.

I was so dead.

"Yeah, that's the reaction I was hoping for," Kayla said, stifling a laugh.

"You're not filming me, are you?" I swatted at her phone. "What's the matter with you? If that ends up on GroupIt, I'll kill you."

"Okay, okay," she said, putting the phone away. She probably realized one dead girl in the room was more than enough.

"What am I going to do?" I sunk down onto the floor.

"The show isn't 'til seven. You still have time to learn the lines. It's just one scene."

"Yeah, one scene of *Shakespeare*!" I was shouting. "I've been trying. Nonstop. That stuff is impossible to learn." I could barely remember the words to my favorite songs. And I liked those! There was no way I could memorize Shakespeare in so little time—it's like a foreign language.

"I'm just going to have to back out," I said.

"You can't do that. Jill will totally kill you. I mean, seriously, she'll take the poison that's meant for Romeo and shove it down your throat. Especially after you begged her for the part."

It was true. Jill *was* going to throw a fit. I told her I'd be the best understudy ever. And I meant to, but every time I tried to learn my lines at rehearsal, I was sent on some stupid Amanda errand. I tried working on them with Dhonielle, but actual work kept getting in the way. And when I tried at home, my eyes just glazed over, and before I knew it time was up.

"Come on, she knows me. There's no way she thinks I learned the part." I wasn't sure if I was trying to convince Kayla or myself.

"Actually, she does."

"Why would she think something so stupid?"

"Because you promised her," Kayla said, leaning back on my dresser. "And you even reassured her last night." She gave me the thumbs-up. The same sign I had given Jill not even twenty-four hours ago.

"You saw that?"

Kayla nodded.

I only did it because I knew Miss Theater-Is-My-Life Amanda Andrews would never miss a performance.

"Jill wasn't even planning to have an understudy," I argued. "So what would she be doing then?"

"Freaking out even more than she already is. I spoke to her this morning, Em," Kayla said. "She's totally counting on you. She wanted to come over here with me and review all her notes with you. She would have, too, if she wasn't stuck babysitting her sister until her mom gets home from the gym."

"Ohhh." I doubled over, holding the lower left side of my stomach. "I think I may need to go to the hospital. I've never felt a pain like this," I moaned, channeling my inner Amanda.

"Ummm, you know appendicitis isn't catching, right?" Kayla asked.

"Whatever. Stranger coincidences have happened than two people having the same disease."

"Know what's even stranger?" Kayla didn't wait for my

answer. "That somehow your appendix wound up on the wrong side."

Shoot. I moved my hands to my right. "The pain is everywhere. Left, right, up, down."

Kayla shook her head. "You really are an awful actress."

"No kidding," I said, dropping the act. "Another reason I can't go on tonight." An awful realization set in. "You know, I wouldn't just be ruining everything for Jill. I'd be ruining everything for *Wes*, too. They're both going to hate me. I have no choice. I have to tell them the truth."

"Then you can kiss the extra credit good-bye."

I bit my lip hard. I desperately needed to cash in on that offer. "I know, but there's nothing I can do. Even if I go up there with the script in my hand, I still won't get the extra credit. All the actors are supposed to have their lines memorized."

Kayla got one of her sneaky little smiles again. "What if we just call up the lines on your phone, and you can just read them? It'll be perfect." She was practically shaking with excitement.

"Except for the fact that it'll be superobvious."

"It won't be. The sleeves on the dress are huge and drape-y. I'll sew in a pocket. You can keep the phone there."

"Won't it be weird that I'm staring at my sleeve the whole time?" I asked.

"It's your first time on stage. Everyone will just think you're nervous," she assured me.

"I *will* be nervous." As much as I wanted the extra credit and to make Jill happy, I couldn't do it. Even if it meant sharing a stage with Wes. "Forget it. The odds of throwing up or fainting are just too high. I don't need to become known as the puke princess of Shaker Heights. I'll just have to pull all As for the rest of the semester."

"In English? You say that as if it were something you knew how to do." Kayla could be a real downer sometimes. She paused for a second. "Look, if you're not going to do it for yourself or for Jill, do it for me," she said.

"*You?*"

"Yes. I made the Juliet dress. It's a shoo-in for best costume. But if you don't do the scene, it won't even be entered."

I'd forgotten all about that. "Kayla, I can't."

"Please?" She put her hands in a little steeple and shook them at me. "Just think how hot you'll look. Wes won't even know what to do with himself."

It *was* a gorgeous dress. A gold corset top and satin skirt with a sheer flowing fabric overlay. I'd been so jealous that Amanda would get to wear it.

"I don't know."

"Come on," she said. "This is the answer to everything. Jill. Wes. My costume. *Your* English grade."

I was pacing my bedroom floor like a madwoman. "You really think I can do it?"

"Absolutely. It's just one scene, and if anyone can pull this off, it's you. You built me a whole website for my designs in *one* day. This is nothing. We'll practice all the way up until the performance, and you'll have the phone for backup."

Maybe she was right. I just needed to get up there and read the lines. I did it at the audition. I could do it now. "All right. I'm in."

"You won't regret this. You'll see."

I just prayed she was right.

11

The dress was at school, so Kayla and I headed over there so she could add in the pocket. We sat up on the balcony built for the *Romeo and Juliet* scene, and I ran through my lines while Kayla sewed. The balcony wasn't very high up, but it still helped set the stage. I actually felt comfortable up there, and as the hours passed, I was getting more confident that this ridiculous plan of ours was going to work! She finished sewing, and I tossed my phone in the pocket for a test. It totally camouflaged it. As I stood up to do a happy dance, Wes walked into the auditorium. I froze midmove.

"Hey," he said, running his hand through his light brown hair.

"Hey," I repeated, and pulled my iPhone back out of the pocket. "You're early."

"Jill wanted us to run through the scene a few times. She should be here any minute."

I glanced at Kayla. I didn't want Jill to know about the phone plan. She'd get extrastressed, which would make me extrastressed, and my performance definitely didn't need that.

"It will be okay," Kayla mouthed to me.

Wes jumped on stage. He was so cute, and his gorgeous brown eyes were totally focused on me. Normally I'd offer up my soul for some extra time with him, but not today. This was just asking for trouble.

He looked up at me on the balcony and smiled. "You're going to make a great Juliet."

"Thanks," I said, smiling back. My mind raced. What did he mean by that? Was he just being nice? Was he flirting with me? Did he know about my massive crush on him and think it was appropriate that I'd play some lovestruck girl?

Did he maybe like me, too?

No way. I couldn't let myself think that . . . at least, not without checking in with Kayla and Jill. Although I knew exactly what they'd say—that I needed to stop overanalyzing *every* little thing Wes Rosenthal said and did. I just needed to talk to him like I'd talk to anyone else. I just needed to be calm. To be breezy.

I could handle that. I'd been doing it every day at rehearsal and in our car rides. Well, as best I could, anyway. "You're going to make a great Romeo, too. I mean, you already are. I mean, I've been watching you perform." *Wait, that sounds creepy.* "Not just you," I quickly added. "I've, y'know . . . been watching everyone. That's what an understudy does. Watch. Well. They learn the lines, too. And watch." *Oh, please stop talking, Emily.* "I mean, an understudy can't just watch a performer. They have to do more than that." *Why can't my mouth stop moving? Or at least start saying something smart?* "And it was a good thing I was cast. With Amanda getting sick and all. She wanted to be here so badly. But I'm here. Well, obviously."

I could tell all my talking was making Wes uncomfortable.

51

That's what it seemed like anyway, but then he just laughed. I couldn't tell if it was real or not. Either way, it was my cue to shut up.

I could feel Kayla's eyes on me in horror. Why hadn't she stopped me? Stomped on my foot, stabbed me with a sewing needle, tossed me off the balcony. Friends were supposed to keep friends from babbling in front of guys they liked.

"She's doing okay, though," Wes said.

"Huh?"

"Amanda. I stopped by the hospital before I came here."

He stopped by the hospital? To see *Amanda*! I bet he took her flowers, too. Did he have a thing for her? She had been flirting with him ever since she and Cody broke up, and he seemed to enjoy it. His feelings were probably even stronger now that she was some damsel in distress. Why couldn't *I* have been the one with my appendix taken out?

"That's cool," I forced myself to say with a smile.

"Yeah, I got a card for everyone to sign. I'll pass it around at the cast party." A card, too? He really was a nice guy.

"That's really sweet of you."

He shrugged. "It's not a big deal."

Maybe not to him. But to me. And I'm sure to Amanda, too. They would definitely be a couple when she got back to school.

The sound of a clap got my attention. It was Jill. "Great, you're both here!" She power walked to the front of the stage. "Em, thank you, thank you, thank you for making me add an understudy. I don't know what I'd be doing right now without you. You totally saved me."

I gave her a small smile. *I could do this, I could do this, I could do this.*

"Okay, how about we run through this baby?" she asked.

I looked at Kayla in panic. I wasn't wearing the dress. How was I supposed to look at my phone without Jill noticing?

"I still need to have her try on the costume, so I can make adjustments," Kayla said, trying to buy me more time.

It didn't work.

"Do that after. We need a run-through." Jill had that don't-mess-with-me voice going on, and her green eyes stared at all of us so intently that it was clear we had no choice.

Kayla put the dress over the banister of the balcony and blocked me from Jill. "Just keep it hidden in the fabric." I did as instructed, and Kayla went and took a seat next to Jill.

"Okay," Jill said, "let's do this."

I took a deep breath and forged ahead with the scene, but I got through only about two lines before Jill jumped right up and interrupted.

"Why are you looking down so much? And what's with all the fidgeting? In the beginning, you should be looking out onto the horizon longingly, thinking about Romeo. And when he says, 'she leans her cheek upon her hand,' you need to put your cheek on your hand! Then when he finally speaks to you—you need to look at him! And try showing a little more emotion. This is supposed to be the guy you love. Let me see it. I want to know you're pining away for him."

I could feel my cheeks starting to burn. I wished Wes wasn't watching me. Any confidence I had before was quickly disappearing. "You're freaking me out, Jill. Can I please just get through this once before you start picking on my performance?"

She pursed her lips. "Fine," she finally said. But I could tell she wasn't happy. Luckily, she just sat back down and kept her mouth shut for the rest of the scene—even when I kept my eyes glued down and fumbled over the words.

It wasn't *my* fault I tripped over the lines. Shakespeare is weird. All those random words—thee, thy, thou, doth—and those were the easy ones.

Kayla clapped for us when we were done. "That was a great first run-through." She was a good liar when she wanted to be. If I hadn't been there myself, I may have actually believed her.

Jill's reaction wasn't quite as positive. Her hands gripped the armrest. "Yeah," she said, trying to force a smile. "But we still have a long way to go."

"And no time to do it," a voice boomed from the back of the auditorium. It was Ryan. He must have come in while I was "performing." "I booked the auditorium until curtain call," he said, a little bossy-sounding if you asked me. "You've got to clear out. My cast is ready."

Yes! Thank you, Ryan. Now I could practice by myself. I rushed down the steps of the stage and made my way for the exit.

"Where do you think you're going?" Jill called after me.

"Home."

"I don't think so," she said. "We're going to run lines backstage."

I looked to Kayla. Without the script in front of me, that was going to be impossible.

"She really needs to try on the costume," Kayla said, coming to my rescue again. "I'll run lines with her. Promise."

Jill clenched her notes tightly. "How about *I* go over the lines with her while *you* work on the dress? Then we'll all be happy."

Letting Jill help wasn't an option. So while I didn't want to hurt her feelings, I didn't have much choice. "I'd rather go over them with Kayla."

Jill's eyes totally popped out of their sockets. "You what?" Her voice was a mix of anger and confusion.

"It's not that I *don't* want you around," I tried to explain. "It's just that I *can't* have you there. You're making me nervous. I know how important this is to you. And I can't focus with you standing over me. You understand, right?"

"Fine," she said, staring at me. "But you better not make me regret this."

I nodded, and Kayla ushered me away before Jill could change her mind.

Wes winked as I passed by. "It'll be okay," he whispered. "We'll totally kill it tonight."

Unfortunately, that was exactly what I was afraid of.

12

I did the scene aloud with Kayla for what seemed like three eternities. "You've totally got this," she said. "You barely checked your phone the last couple of times, and that last read-through sounded great."

"You need a new definition of *great*," I told her.

"Look, you don't need to be Laurence Olivier—"

"Who?"

"He was a great Shakespearean actor, but it doesn't matter. What I meant was, you don't have to give an award-winning performance. Everyone knows you didn't have much rehearsal time; they're going to cut you a lot of slack. You just need to get through the scene, and you can do that. Now come on, let's get you in costume."

I kept reciting lines as Kayla pulled the Juliet gown over my head.

"O Romeo, Romeo! Wherefore art thou Romeo? Deny thy father and refuse thy name." I was starting to feel overheated. "Can we open the door?" I asked as she laced up the dress's bodice. "It's stuffy in here."

We had been in the dressing room forever, and I felt totally cooped up. "Ow," I said as Kayla gave the ribbons a tug.

"Sorry, I'm just trying to get it to close. It's a little tighter on you than Amanda."

"Thanks a lot."

"I didn't say that was a bad thing," Kayla said, pulling some more. "It just means I need to pull a little harder to get it to close all the way in the back."

"Okay, but I won't be able to say the lines if I can't breathe."

"But it will make your boobs look really good. You'll have killer cleavage in this thing." Kayla gave another giant tug.

"I'd prefer not to pass out or have my lungs collapse."

"Yeah, yeah, yeah," she said.

I let out a gasp.

"What? Did I really pull too hard? Are you okay?"

"Look. Straight. Ahead," I whispered.

"Oh, Romeo! Oh, Romeo!" she said, and gave a little growl. "Talk about a view."

"Shhh!" I warned her. But she was right. I was having trouble breathing again, but this time it had nothing to do with the dress and everything to do with Wes Rosenthal.

He was standing in the dressing room across from us, shirt-less, and looking completely . . .

Oh.

My.

God.

Hot.

I'd never seen muscles like that. I knew I probably should've looked away, but I couldn't. Sure, I'd seen Wes without a shirt when we were kids, but this was a whole new level. And while there'd been the occasional shirtless pic on GroupIt over the years, the live version was soooo much better. I couldn't take my eyes off him. He was the dizzying, just-got-off-the-spinning-teacups-ride kind of handsome. I mean, he seriously looked incredible. He still had a hint of a tan from his Florida trip, and he had a solid six-pack. *Six!* I wondered what it would be like to trace my fingers around his muscles.

"I think you're drooling," Kayla whispered in my ear.

"Ha-ha."

"Thirty minutes to places," Jill called as she made her way backstage. I quickly looked at my feet so Wes wouldn't catch me staring.

"Whoa," Jill said when she saw him. "Sorry, I didn't know you were still changing."

"It's okay. I don't care," he said.

Jill quickly averted her eyes from him anyway and turned to me. "Do you see this?" she silently mouthed to me. Did I see it? Of course I saw it! I was drunk off it. Although I was smitten before I saw him shirtless. This was just a cherry on top. A really nice, yummy cherry—but a cherry all the same. "We're up first," Jill said, gaining her composure. "Break a leg. And, Em, thank you again for stepping in."

"Yeah," Wes said. "We'll have fun out there. And you look great, by the way."

I looked great?! He really said that. To *me*! "Thanks. There are no tissues this time," I said, and gestured toward my chest.

"What?" Jill mouthed to me, and Kayla snorted.

"Ohhhhkaaaay," Kayla said in a singsong voice. "Time for Emily to finish doing her hair," she said with a wave before closing the dressing room door in an attempt to save me. "No tissues? Seriously, Em?"

"I panicked. He said I looked great, and my chest is practically up to my nose in this getup, so it was the first thing that popped into my head."

"Next time, you might just want to stick with 'thank you' or 'you too.' "

"Now you tell me."

"Don't worry about it," she said, and pulled back a strand of hair from each side of my face and tied them together in the back. "You have more important things to think about now."

That was definitely true. In less than a half hour, I was going to be standing in front of an audience.

The minutes flew by, and before I knew it, it was time.

"You can do this. Remember, if you get stuck, just use your phone, it's in place," Kayla said as she adjusted the fabric on my dress one last time before I headed out on stage.

I nodded. Like it or not, I, Emily Stein, was about to make my theatrical debut. *Please let this go smoothly*, I prayed.

The lights turned on, and Wes began to speak. He really made Shakespeare sound good. Although he could have recited the *Barney & Friends* theme song and I still would have been impressed. But it wasn't just Wes up there. It was me, too.

Okay, I told myself. *Time to act. Make Jill proud.*

I looked out longingly and fantasized about Wes telling me he loved me. I even managed to lean on the banister and remembered to touch my hand to my cheek. And then on top of all that, I got out my first line without looking at my phone. Okay, fine, it was just "Ay me!"—but it was still something. Maybe this wasn't going to be so bad after all. And Wes really did look adorable in his costume—the tunic, the puffy sleeves, even the tights. The whole getup sounded ridiculous, but somehow he managed to pull it off. His broad shoulders helped. And his calf muscles. And his perfect jawline. He was basically what I imagined a Greek god would look like. But I had to stop thinking about Wes. I had lines to say.

"O Romeo, Romeo! Wherefore art thou Romeo?" I recited from memory. All those run-throughs with Kayla must have paid off. I was actually remembering the words. "Deny thy father and refuse thy name; or, if thou wilt not, be but sworn my love, and I'll no longer be a Capulet." I made it through my first tough part without even glancing down. This was actually a little fun, if that was at all possible.

"Shall I hear more, or shall I speak at this?" Wes said.

His line was an aside, which meant I wasn't technically supposed to hear it, or in this case, even know he was there, but when I heard his voice, I couldn't help but look over. It was kind of an instinct.

Wes saw me looking and gave me a little wink and a nod, and I felt a surge go through me. It was just the two of us up there. It felt really nice. I could picture us afterward laughing and dancing at the cast party, maybe even sharing a kiss. But I couldn't think about that now. I needed to keep going with the scene. But then I made a mistake. A huge one. I looked away from Wes and out to the audience. There were a LOT of people out there. Every seat was filled. And they were waiting for me to speak. I looked back at Wes, but the vision of all those eyes on me kept playing over and over. I went to say my next line, but it was gone. There was no Shakespeare left in my brain. It had been replaced with pure panic.

I needed to relax. To take a deep breath. I breathed in, but it was as if the air was caught in my throat. Why couldn't I breathe? I actually felt dizzy. *Duh, Emily.* Of course I did. I was wearing a freaking corset. You couldn't take deep breaths in that. I tried to regain my composure. I saw Wes watching me. He looked concerned. That was totally breaking character. I couldn't ruin this for him. I could do it. I just needed to follow the plan. I needed to forget the idea of magically remembering every word Juliet was supposed to say and just read the lines from my phone. That's what it was there for.

I slightly lifted my arm, pressed my thumb on the phone to turn it back on—and it started buzzing! *What the . . . ?* Who was texting me now? I glanced down at the screen.

NOOOOOOOOO!!!!!!!

It was a battery alert. I hadn't charged my phone during all of those rehearsals with Kayla. I was down to 1 percent. What did that mean? How long did I have? It couldn't be much time. I had no choice. I had to race through my lines.

"'Tis but thy name that is my enemy; thou art thyself, though not a Montague. What's Montague? It is nor hand, nor foot," I said at a crazy warp speed, before the alert popped up again. *NO! I did not want to turn off my phone or switch to low-power mode. I just wanted it to work.*

I cleared the message and kept going. "Nor arm, nor face, nor any other part . . ."

It buzzed again, and that annoying picture of the battery with just the tiniest sliver of power remained. *Just show me my lines.* Why had I been so stupid? How could I have not thought to charge my phone?

I was a disaster. Speeding then stopping abruptly. But

what other choice did I have? I just had to get to where it was Wes's turn to speak.

I swiped the alert away again. I couldn't even remember where I left off. "Nor face, nor any other part belonging to a—"

Then my heart stopped. Okay, not really. But my phone did, and at that moment, my phone's dying felt almost just as bad.

No, no, no, no, NO!!! *What was I going to do?*

There were no more lines for me to read. Just whatever I could come up with, and that obviously was nothing!

I couldn't just stand there. Silence was deadly. I had to do something. And before I knew it I was humming. "Hmmm, hmmm, hmmm. Romeo, Romeo, Romeo." Oh, I sounded dumb. Maybe silence was better. The whispers in the audience were starting. *Think, Emily. Think.* "Hmmm, hmmm, hmmm." I had no choice. I had to improvise. I had to make up the lines. I understood the gist of the passage: It was about Romeo and Juliet being enemies because their families were feuding . . . and that if they had different last names, it wouldn't be such a big deal. I just needed to turn that into Shakespeare. *Quickly.*

Shakespeare just added a bunch of *th*s and *st*s at the end of words and threw in some *methinks* and *doths*. I could do that, too. No big deal.

"'Tis but my name that's the problem, so I will doth give-est it up-eth to be with thou. Or you could give-est up-eth yours. I mean thou's."

I could hear light snickers and giggles from the crowd.

"Huh?" someone asked, a little too loudly for my taste.

And then I heard it. A groan. An I-told-you-not-to-disappoint-me groan. A Jill groan. She was definitely going to decapitate me later. The only thing scarier than the thought of that was the look on Wes's face. His eyes were wide, and he was staring at me as if I'd flung a baseball at his head.

I gave a small wave.

"Hi-eth, Romeo," I said, figuring I'd jump ahead to the part where Juliet saw him. Anything to speed up the disaster I'd created.

"Hi-eth," he answered back. I couldn't even fathom what he was thinking right now.

"So glad thou are here-est," I said.

Some guy's voice rang out from the crowd. "What is she saying?" he asked.

But I couldn't stop. The show had to go on.

"Romeo," I continued, "how did-est thou find-est moi?" Great . . . now I was speaking French.

Wes seemed to have recovered from the shock of my curveball and recited the next line. "Alack, there lies more peril in thine eye than twenty of their swords." Well, that was true. I certainly had peril in my eyes. I was dying a slow, embarrassing death on stage. "Look thou but sweet," he continued, "and I am proof against their enmity."

He sounded so good. I wished I could keep up, but sadly, I had no idea what my response was supposed to be.

"If they do see thee, they will murder thee," a harsh whisper called out. It was Kayla. *Thank God.*

"If they do see thee, they will murder thee," I repeated.

Okay, this could work. I'd just let her feed me lines. Wes said something else. And then I heard Kayla whispering again, but I couldn't make out what she was saying.

"Can you repeat-eth that, Romeo?" I asked. "Thou voice-eth need-est to be LOUDER-ETH."

Someone in the audience snorted, and Jill muttered, "This isn't happening." Unfortunately for both of us, it was.

I looked out at the crowd. Some girl in the front row had her hand over her mouth. Samara Lowry was whispering something in Bridgette Riley's ear, no doubt about me. And the entire audience had its eyes glued to the stage, waiting to see what I'd do next. The only good thing was that my parents weren't there. I was smart enough not to tell them about this little train wreck of a performance.

I stood there like a lump, waiting for my line. Finally, I turned toward Kayla and repeated, "I said, LOUDER-ETH."

She fed me the line again. Supercrazy loud this time. "I would not for the world."

It was so loud, the crowd heard it and started to laugh. Not the snickers from before, but those evil, full belly laughs people get when watching home videos of someone getting kicked in the groin. Wes was going to hate me for putting him through this. This torture needed to end.

"Methinks," I said, "I could use-eth a book-eth." *Come on, Kayla. Take the hint.* "You know-eth. A BOOK-ETH where-est I can recite-eth beauteous words to thee . . . thou . . . whatever. I NEED THE BOOK-ETH."

As I was shouting that last *book-eth*, I got my wish. The script came sailing from off stage left and hit me in the back of the head. "Ow," I unintentionally yelled, to the delight of the crowd. It weighed a ton.

"Sorry," Kayla whispered. "My bad."

I didn't care. I'd get over the pain faster than the embarrassment I was suffering. I was just happy to have the script. At least I was until I realized Kayla hadn't bookmarked the page

I needed. It was the *complete* works of Shakespeare. There was no way I would find the right page. Not to mention that since the book was with me, Kayla couldn't even feed me lines anymore. R&J wasn't a tragedy. My life was.

I was so flunking English.

"Would thou like some help, my sweet Juliet?"

Did Wes just call me sweet? I swung around to face him, but I wasn't paying attention to where I was stepping and my foot went right off the balcony. Wes lunged forward to catch me, but why would anything go right for me? So instead of Wes stopping me from hitting the floor, I took him down with me.

I was lying on top of Wes Rosenthal. Only, this was not like any of my daydreams. This was mortifying. I rolled off him and jumped up. "Are you okay?" I was visibly shaking.

Wes stood up, too. "Don't worry-eth, Juliet," he said without any anger in his voice. He even smiled at me. For a second I thought that meant he didn't hate me for the craziness I was causing. But then I remembered he was acting. He actually took what he was doing seriously, and right now his part called for him to be in love with Juliet.

Wes said some line I assumed was to get us back on track. But I had no response. I couldn't take it anymore. The laughter of the audience. The panic coursing through my body. The thought of making Wes suffer more. It needed to end.

So I did the only thing I could think of—something super-Elizabethan. I put the back of my hand to my forehead, pretended to swoon, and let my whole body fall back to the ground with a loud thump.

"I am so sorry-eth, Romeo."

"It's okay." He sat down on the ground next to me and took my hand. I felt little sparks fly through me.

I shook my head. I couldn't let him go through this anymore. "No, I know how-eth this play end-eth. I think I shall stab-eth myself now to save-eth us both."

"Finally," someone in the audience yelled out.

I picked up an imaginary dagger and began to plunge it into my heart.

"No," Wes said, stopping me before I committed imaginary suicide. "Our story is not over yet. So let's just say, 'Parting is such sweet sorrow, that I shall say good night 'til it be morrow.'"

I was pretty sure that was supposed to be my line. But I decided I probably shouldn't point that out. Then he stood up and walked off the stage.

After a moment, someone finally took mercy on me and brought the stage lights down.

The scene was over. But I knew all too well that my embarrassment was just beginning.

13

"There you are!" Kayla said. "I've been looking for you everywhere."

I'd been hiding in a dressing room since the scene ended. There was no way I was going back on stage—not for a bow or to hear them read the nominees for best actress.

"Is it over?"

"Yep," she said, and held up a little trophy that had BEST COSTUME DESIGNER written on it. "I won!"

"Congratulations."

"Hey," she said. "You could sound a little more excited."

"Seriously? After what just happened out there?"

Kayla sat down next to me. "Yeah, that was bad." I could tell she was trying to hold back a giant smile. "But people will forget about it."

I just looked at her. At least February break started Monday. I wouldn't have to deal with anyone for a week.

"Okay," she conceded, "maybe they won't forget anytime soon. But come on, it *was* kind of funny."

"For you, maybe." I dropped my head onto the makeup table. "You know, for a second there I actually thought I knew the lines. I totally screwed up. What a mess. Jill's—" I bolted upright. "Where is Jill?"

"Still in the auditorium."

"I need to get out of here now."

"You have to talk to her sometime," Kayla reminded me.

"I know that. I'm going to apologize. I just prefer to do it when she's had some time to cool down. I gotta go."

"Fine." Kayla tossed me my purse and my phone, which I had been charging nearby. "We can head to the cast party now."

"Very funny. There's no way I'm going to that. Not only will Jill be there but so will Wes." The thought of what I did to him made me cringe. I covered my face with my hands. It was definitely burning up. I was probably stop-sign red. "I should just move out of the state. Wes is going to hate me. I won't be able to look him in the eye ever again. I'm going to die of embarrassment. I can't handle being in the same room as him."

"You're going," Kayla said.

I dropped my hands and looked at her. "Are you crazy? No, I'm not."

"Yeah, you are," she said. "The best way to get past this is to face it. This will help you."

"You and I have very different definitions of *help*," I said. "Going to that party will be torture. Everyone is going to rip into me. I can't do it."

"I know you, Em." Kayla put her arm around me. "You'll have to deal with these people sometime, and the longer you put it off, the longer you're going to be stressing over it and trying to avoid it. Might as well get it out of the way now, when you can have me by your side."

"I probably won't even be allowed in," I reasoned. "Mrs. Heller probably wants to flunk me out of school right about now." Which, honestly, sounded better than having to see anyone again.

"Just tell her you had a horrible case of stage fright. After all, what you did up there was pretty frightening."

I rolled my eyes at her. "Thanks."

"But seriously, Em. The party is not going to be any worse than what you already went through. You need to just get it over with."

"I don't know . . ."

"I can always call Jill," Kayla said, "and tell her to come meet us in the dressing room."

"You wouldn't."

"Oh, you know I would," she said.

"Fine. You win. I'll go to the cast party."

"That's my girl," she said. "You'll be thanking me later."

I highly doubted that would be the case, but even so, I made my way to what was undoubtedly going to be the cast party from hell.

14

I braced for the worst as we approached The Heights, where the party was being held. I imagined everyone was waiting for me to get there so they could point and laugh as one big collective group. But when I walked into the student center, no one seemed to notice. They were all busy talking and scarfing down pizza and pop. And the coast seemed clear of both Jill and Wes, at least for the moment.

"See, it's not so bad," Kayla said, squeezing my arm. "Everyone's focused on celebrating their own performances and scenes, they're not even thinking about yours."

But she jinxed us. No sooner had the last word spilled from her lips than Ryan Watkins strode over, clutching his best director trophy. "You know, Em . . ." He tossed the metal statue from one hand to the other. "I could have won this on my own. You didn't need to sabotage poor Jill. I appreciate it, but it really wasn't necessary."

That one stung. I really needed to apologize to Jill. But tomorrow, after things settled a little. "Ha-ha," I said to Ryan, making sure to sound as monotone as possible. But he was just the start of it. His approach opened the floodgates.

Mason Noland and Omar Jothy, two of Wes's buddies from the lacrosse team, came over next.

"Man, do we owe you," Mason said, putting his hand on my shoulder. "Our boy is never going to live this down. He thought he was going to get flak for the tunic and tights—"

"Hey," Kayla said. "There was nothing wrong with that tunic. It looked hot. And I used the same pants our football players wear, so unless you have something to say to guys who are twice your size, I think you should lay off my costumes."

Mason put up his hands in defense. "I'm just saying his clothes are the least of his worries." He winked at me. "You gave us material that will follow him to the grave."

"Look-eth!" Omar pointed at my face. "Emily-eth is turning red-eth."

I stuck out my tongue at him.

"I'd watch out, O. If you don't stop, she may pull out her invisible dagger and come at you." Mason then pretended to plunge a knife deep into his chest.

"Give it a rest, guys," Kayla said, coming to my defense.

"Emily knows we're kidding," he answered as he pretended to pull out the dagger and hand it to me with a slight bow. I accepted graciously. I knew they didn't mean any harm. Truth was, if I hadn't messed up everything for Wes and Jill, I'd probably be laughing at myself, too.

Jace Brennan came over and slapped his teammates on their backs. "Hmmm, hmmm, hmmm. Whatever could you guys be talking about?"

"Don't you start," Kayla warned her boyfriend.

"Wouldn't dream of it." He moved over to her and planted a light kiss on her lips.

He might have meant it, but Omar and Mason looked as if they were just warming up. Kayla saw it, too. "All right, you've had your fun. Time to give Emily a break. Looks like they put out some more pizza. Why don't you guys go check it out?"

She didn't need to tell them twice; they were all over the food in twenty seconds.

They might have left, but others took their place. Over the next ten minutes, three of my classmates pretended to faint in front of me, four imitated my Shakespeare-speak, and I caught about a dozen others looking at me and laughing. The only upside was that there hadn't been any Jill or Wes sightings.

Just when I thought I'd had about as much as I could take, part of the cast from the *A Midsummer Night's Dream* scene came over. Including Dhonielle. "Way to steal our thunder," she said, faking a pout and crossing her arms.

"Yeah, we were supposed to have the funniest scene tonight," J.J. Pickford joined in. "You know how hard you were to follow?"

"I personally feel like I should be handing over my best actress in a comedy award to you," Sari Lawson added.

"Nah," Dhonielle said, giving me a light jab with her elbow, "you keep it. I wouldn't call what Emily did acting, per se."

"I don't know," J.J. said, rubbing his chin, "some of the best actors are improvisers. You should know that! And Shakespeare was all about entertaining the crowd, which Emily certainly did."

"And made myself a laughingstock in the process," I added.

"Who cares?" Sari said. "It sucks now, but some day you're going to look back and laugh. At our fifty-year reunion, when we've forgotten who half of these people are, everyone will remember you and smile. That's more than most of us can say."

"Infamy, woo-hoo," I said, and whirled my finger around.

"Okay," Dhonielle said, smacking my finger away. "If this was anyone else getting all depressed about doing something ridiculous, I'd get it. But you? You're the one who makes up ridiculous games to play at work and sings Taylor Swift songs over the loudspeaker after the grocery store closes, and on a dare did it during store hours. I've heard you sing. If there's anything you should be embarrassed about, that kind of takes the cake."

"I guess . . ." But the difference with the singing was I chose to do that and it was supposed to be a joke, while the Shakespeare mishap was anything but intentional. And it involved me humiliating Wes and screwing over Jill.

"No, 'I guess.' You know I'm right. And in the immortal words of Taylor Swift, you need to . . ." She gestured for me to continue.

"Shake it off," I filled in.

"Exactly."

Then Dhonielle, Sari, and J.J. started jumping around and singing while Kayla and I kind of stood awkwardly watching. Theater people didn't mind being the center of attention, but I personally had my fill for the week, maybe even for the century. At least they made me feel better.

"Thanks, guys," I said as they shook their way to the drinks.

I let out a deep breath. "There, I did it. I faced the music, now can I go?"

"It hasn't even been a half hour," Kayla said.

I looked toward the door. Another group had just walked in. And I couldn't miss that swath of red hair and those freckles right in the middle. It was Jill. "Okay, you convinced me. I'll stay, but I gotta go say hi to someone. I'll see you in a bit."

"But . . ."

I didn't wait to hear what she had to say. I booked it to the other side of the room. There was no way I was facing Jill right there in the middle of everyone. I took a seat at a table in the back corner. There were a bunch of people standing in front of it, so I figured they'd make good cover. To be extrasafe, I sunk down in my chair. If I could just lie low for a bit, I could sneak out when Jill was away from the exit.

With nothing else to do, I pulled out my phone. It wasn't like I really wanted to know what everyone was posting about me, but I couldn't help but open GroupIt anyway. Uckkk. I didn't even know you could get two hundred plus notifications over the course of a few hours, but apparently my classmates loved sharing, commenting on, and favoriting my embarrassing moments. I was afraid to see how many posts there would be by tomorrow. It was like the jabs from this party in bulk—only in writing. Not to mention the added benefit of pictures, gifs, videos, and Vines.

How did I let myself do something so stupid? I knew I'd be asking myself that question for a long, long time. I wished I were in some sci-fi novel where I could just be sucked into some alternate dimension—one where I had learned my lines and gave an amazing performance.

I wasn't so lucky. At least my blending into the wall seemed to keep people away. No one came up to me for about twenty minutes. But then something horrible happened. I looked up, and Jill was headed in my direction from the left. I wanted to run right, but that wasn't safe, either! Wes was over that way, and he was walking toward me, too.

This was bad. I was trapped. Which way was I supposed to go? I didn't even know Wes was here. Wouldn't I have seen him before this? I figured he had skipped the party to avoid the ridicule. Why put yourself through this if you didn't have someone like Kayla forcing you to attend? But just my luck, he showed up.

Now I had an impossible decision. Jill. Wes. Jill. Wes. Neither option seemed good. I wasn't ready to face either of them. There was a possibility that neither saw me, and I could just get up, walk past them, and they'd never notice. But given the kind of day I was having, the odds of that working out seemed incredibly low.

If I couldn't go left and I couldn't go right, I had to stay put. Only, I couldn't let them spot me. I had to escape. I didn't have any other choice. There was only one way out: I would have to go under the table.

I slid down and prayed the tablecloth would be enough of a cover. *Was I really doing this?*

Please let them just walk by. Please let them just walk by.

I thought I was safe, but then I heard a knock on the table.

I froze. Who was it? *Anyone but Wes or Jill. Anyone but Wes or Jill.*

"Hello? Is someone there?"

No, no, no, no, NO. It was Wes. Why couldn't it have been Ryan? I would have taken more of his stupid comments. Anything but this. This was worse than the Shakespeare scene. I did not want him to find me cowering under a table. Had my life actually come to this? Me ducking for cover at a school party? What was next? Lunch in the bathroom stall?

But I couldn't worry about any of that right now. Wes was too close. Chances were good he would just think he'd been mistaken and hadn't seen me there. Or that I'd gotten up before he'd made it over. Once he'd left, I'd sneak out. Or maybe I'd just stay hidden away there until Kayla texted me she was ready to leave. As I considered my options, one side of the tablecloth began to lift.

"Emily?" Wes asked, peering under the table.

I banged my head as I looked up to see him.

"Are you okay?"

"Yeah," I said, rubbing what was probably going to be a really big bump. "Doesn't hurt that much." I tried to blink back the pain.

"What were you doing down there?"

"Ummm, earring," I said.

He squinted in confusion, and I realized I'd been caught in a lie. I was wearing both earrings. I touched my left earlobe. "I was lucky I found it." I tried to smile. "You know, the floor is cleaner than I'd imagined." I patted the ground for good measure.

Why was I talking about the floor? And why was I still sitting there? I probably should have gotten up, but then I'd *really* have to face him. And by this point, in for a penny, in for a pound. I just needed him to drop the tablecloth and walk away. But he wasn't budging. Great. *Say something smart, Emily.* Make him leave. "So . . ." was as far as I got. My mind totally blanked. I could not think of one halfway intelligent thing to say. I just sat there gawking at him gawking at me. I don't think he knew what to make of the whole situation. Or the way I was acting. Not that I could blame him.

This conversation, or lack thereof, was more painful than hitting my head. I would have preferred that he ream me out for making him look like a fool today, rather than just look at me still sitting there. I *really* needed to do something. Then I got it. What I should have done all along. Apologize.

"I'm sorry about today," I said. "I never meant to mess that up for you. It was because . . ." My voice trailed off. I didn't have a good reason for why it happened.

He dropped the tablecloth and left me in the dark. He didn't want to hear my excuse. He was leaving. Well, that was what I wanted, right? But somehow it made me feel worse.

But then he was there. WES WAS CRAWLING UNDER THE TABLE WITH ME!

First, I saw his face, then the rest of him. His whole body was scrunched up next to mine. He had to crouch his head down. He was rather tall, and the table wasn't that high.

"Hi," he said, and gave me a smile that showed off his dimple.

I was a little stunned. "Hi," I managed to get out. *What was he doing under here?*

His eyes caught mine, and I felt that rush I always got around him. Without looking away, he said, "I'm glad I found you. I've been looking for you."

What?! After all that, he wanted to see me?! A wave of relief washed over my body. Maybe Kayla and Dhonielle had been right. Maybe this wasn't as big a deal as I was making it out to be. Maybe I hadn't blown my chance with Wes. "Yeah?" I questioned.

"Yeah. I was worried you might be upset over the scene," he said.

Why was he being so nice? "Maybe just a little," I told him, then I held my arms all the way out to show I meant a lot. After all, I was still hiding under a table. It was obvious I wasn't doing too well.

"You know it's going to be okay, right? You don't have to hide from people," he said, his gaze still squarely on me. He knew I was lying about the earring, and he didn't care.

"But I screwed up so bad. I ruined it for you. . . ."

"No, you didn't. I still got the extra credit. And, come on, it was kind of funny." He nudged my shoulder with his.

"I don't know about that."

"You know how to make people laugh," he said. "It's a good thing. The only thing more epic than today was your bat mitzvah party."

I cringed. I had forgotten about that. At the time, I thought a lip-sync battle would be fun, and for my turn, I put together a through-the-decades montage, which had me doing snippets of songs from the fifties, sixties, seventies, eighties, nineties, 2000s, and beyond, complete with outlandish costumes. "That was planned, though. It wasn't *acting*."

"It was still pretty awesome. I was jealous I hadn't thought of something like that for mine."

I definitely remembered his bar mitzvah. At the party, everyone was dancing as a group. Then a slow song came on. For a split second I thought he was going to ask me to dance; and if he didn't, I decided I was going to ask him. But then Elyssa Drayer beat me to the punch, and they were together for two whole years after that. "Really?"

"Yeah. And you'll get through this unscathed, too. You know everyone likes you."

How was he always able to make me feel better? Maybe today wasn't going as horribly as I thought.

"And if it helps, you're not alone. We're in this together. Okay?" Then he gave me one of his little winks.

I may have liked Wes before, but now I knew I loved him.

"Now let's get out from under here." He crawled out and reached his hand out for mine.

I was HOLDING WES ROSENTHAL'S HAND.

Sure, it was just because he was helping me stand up, but who cared?! Did I have to ever let go?

My moment of bliss didn't last long, because my emergence from the protective layer of the tablecloth did not go unnoticed.

"EMILY!" Jill's roar came from about ten feet away.

"Oh, God," I said, half under my breath. I dropped Wes's hand and clung to the table. Was it too late to go back under there?

"How could you do that to me?" she asked, storming over.

"It wasn't—" Wes started to answer.

"Wes," Jill hissed. "This is not about you. Can you please give us a minute?"

"It's okay," I said, and nodded at him to go. I wanted him to save himself; and he wasn't stupid, he took off. If I could have escaped, I would have gone for it, too.

"Jill, I am so sorry."

"And instead of just saying that, you decided to avoid me?"

She was glaring at me, and I totally deserved it. She was right. "I didn't know what to say. I thought maybe things wouldn't look so bad tomorrow. I was planning to stop by your house before I went to work. I was even planning to bring flowers and ice cream—coffee toffee, your favorite."

"You can't buy your way out of this."

"I know. You're right."

She crossed her arms over her chest. "You PROMISED that you could do this. Did you even try to learn the lines? You knew how important this was to me, and now Ryan is going to lord this over my head forever."

"I know. I feel awful. I'm so, so, so, so sorry. Please, you have to forgive me. I'll do whatever it takes to make it up to you. You have to know how bad I feel."

She didn't say anything. She just continued to give me her signature don't-mess-with-me stare, which I took as a sign to keep groveling. "I never meant to ruin everything for you. I tried to learn the lines. Really. But with that history project and those extra shifts at Northside so I could save up for a car, and Amanda making me her gopher, I just got overwhelmed. I swear, I never thought I'd wind up on stage or I would have memorized them. Even if it meant giving up sleep or car money. Please say something." I grabbed her hands.

She pulled them back. "Why didn't you just tell me?"

"Because I'm an idiot."

At that point, Kayla joined us, and Jill pointed her finger at her. "Don't think that I don't know you were in on this. You could have warned me what was going on, too, you know." Kayla's eyes darted to the ground, and she started playing with the ends of her long, dark braid.

"It's not her fault," I said. "She was just trying to help. I really thought I'd be able to pull it off."

Jill was seriously fuming. I wished I had a cute kitten or Seth Werner, Jill's current crush, to distract her. I seriously considered yelling out to see if Seth was in the room. But without those options, I decided to just spill it all. "I didn't want to disappoint you—or lose the extra credit points," I cringed at my confession, "so I had my lines on my phone. But it died. And I thought I might have had them memorized. I spent all day trying. Really. But then"—I saw we had a few spectators, so I lowered my voice—"*he* winked at me, and I looked at the crowd, and there were so many people. And I couldn't breathe in that dress. No offense, Kayla. And then I just tried to salvage the scene the best way I could, which I know didn't work.

"Jill, tell me what I can do to make it up to you," I pleaded. "I'll do it. I'm serious." I raised my right hand. "I, Emily Stein, solemnly swear to do whatever Jillian Frankel wants until she forgives me. Anything. Babysit your sister for you. Create you the best web page ever. Make you my super-duper everything-and-more chocolate-chip cookies. You know no one bakes like I do."

She just shook her head at me.

"Tell me what I can do to fix this."

She didn't say anything. We just stood there in silence. It was probably only for fifteen seconds, but it felt like fifteen weeks.

"I'm so sorry," my voice came out as a whisper, and my head was swimming. It was bad enough I looked like a colossal fool in front of a good portion of the town, but if I lost one of my best friends because of it, too, I'd never forgive myself. "I will make this up to you. Honest."

Her expression softened ever so softly. "You could have told me the truth."

"From now on. Always."

"Me too," Kayla piped in.

"Please forgive me," I begged some more.

"Well," Jill said, a small smile forming on her face, "it's not like I would have won best director with you as my Juliet anyway. You never really had a chance to work on the scene."

"Does this mean we're okay?" I asked.

She paused and then nodded. "I'm still mad, but we're okay-eth."

"Really? Thank you," I said, and gave her a huge hug. Kayla joined in, too.

"I guess after the humiliation you suffered today, I could give you a break," she said, and shook her head. "You outdid yourself this time, Em. That was the biggest train wreck I've ever seen."

"But it was funny," Kayla added. "My favorite was, 'A book-eth where-est I can recite-eth beauteous words.'" She started laughing, and it was kind of contagious.

Jill broke into a wide, toothy grin. "That was painfully wonderful." She shook her head at me. "Or when Kayla flung the script at you and that look on your face. Or when you fell on top of Wes . . ."

She burst into such hysterics she couldn't even get out any more words.

"That humming," Kayla jumped in, she herself doubled over in laughter. "'Hmmm, hmmm, hmmm. Romeo, Romeo, Romeo.' That was awesome."

"Glad you both find my humiliation so humorous." But I

was laughing, too. Everything was good again. Sure, I made a complete joke of myself in front of the whole school, but I had my two best friends by my side (I was 100 percent going to make it up to Jill) and the boy of my dreams saying we were in it together. All in all, it wasn't such a bad day.

"Let's get out of here. I'll give you guys a ride," Jill said, and put one arm around me. Kayla did the same on the other side. Then they gave each other a look, and somewhere between laughing fits, they started humming.

I was serenaded to a chorus of "hmmm, hmmm, hmmm, Em, Em, Em" as we made our way to the car.

15

"Emily," my mother called up to me.

I rubbed my eyes and looked at the alarm clock. It was nine thirty in the morning. "I'm sleeping," I yelled back. I was on vacation. February break meant sleeping in. And it was my last chance, too. Tomorrow was back to school.

"You used up all the milk."

Shoot. I had been up all night making Jill I'm-so-sorry cookies. I know she said she forgave me, but I was serious about making it up to her. I had already taken over ice cream and that new dystopian book she had been dying to read. Cookies were just the next step in my plan.

"I'll get it later. I promise," I called down to the kitchen.

"I need it now."

Why now? It was early. I dragged myself out of bed and made my way down to her. "I'm tired. I'll go at one."

"And how am I supposed to make this?"

Macaroni, butter, cheese, and a bunch of other things were spread over the counter. I forgot my parents had a potluck that night, and their contribution was Mom's famous mac and cheese.

Her hand was gripping the back of her neck. "Your father has the car. I have a conference call soon. I don't have time to walk to the store and back, make this, do the call and still get ready."

"Fine. I'll go now," I said, heading her off before I got another lecture about responsibility and consideration. I grabbed my purse from the table and threw on my sneakers. "You can get ready and do your other stuff. I'll even make it for you. It doesn't take very long. Okay?"

"Thank you," she said, the muscles in her face starting to relax.

"I'll be back soon." I opened the door to the garage.

"Wait." She looked me up and down. "You can't go out like that."

I glanced at my reflection in the window. I wasn't that bad. Okay, I wasn't great. I had a serious case of bed head, the T-shirt I was wearing was too tight and had a golf ball–size hole to the left of my belly button, and my sweats were an old pair of my mom's from before she dropped sixty pounds and were way too big on me. The crotch was basically at my knees. But I was picking up milk, I wasn't trying out for *America's Next Top Model*. I'd be in and out. My coworkers wouldn't think anything of it. It wasn't like I wore my Sunday best to work—not when I spent a good portion of my day in the storage room. And I didn't care if a bunch of old people or new parents, who were pretty much the only ones shopping at this hour, thought I looked like a sewer rat. I was not Amanda. I didn't need to dress to the nines just to make a five-minute stop. I wasn't that vain.

And if I didn't care what I looked like, my mom certainly

shouldn't. "It's nine thirty in the morning. Nobody I want to impress will be at the market."

"But, Emily . . ."

"Do you want the milk or not?" I asked.

She held up her hands. "Fine. Do what you want."

I jumped on my bike and headed to the store. It was a little chilly out. I should have put on a coat. If I had a car, this wouldn't have been an issue. Days like this made having only one vehicle for the whole family particularly annoying.

Fortunately, I didn't live too far from the store, so I was there in less than fifteen minutes. I locked up my bike and went inside.

Dhonielle was bagging groceries and waved at me when I walked in. "Nice hair," she said.

"Thank you, it matches my outfit. I call it euro chic grunge à la bed head."

"You may start a trend."

"That's my goal."

Dhonielle handed two sacks to her customer, a woman in her sixties or so, and then turned back to me. "What are you doing here?"

"What? Aren't you glad to see me?"

"Always," she said. "But I thought you worked last night?"

"I did. I just need to pick up something for my mom."

Another customer began checking out, so I told Dhonielle I'd catch her on my way out and headed to the dairy section in the back.

I just made it there when I heard the loudspeaker go off. It was Dhonielle. "Ms. Stein, please report to the office, stat. Ms. Stein, please report to the office, stat. Hurry."

Huh? I wasn't sure if she was trying to prank me or what. I had just spoken to her a minute ago and said I'd be back. What could be so urgent? Then something caught my eye: the mirrored globe thing in the corner that covered the security camera. Someone was walking in my direction. And it wasn't just any someone.

It was *Wes*.

Dhonielle was trying to get me into hiding because I looked like a goblin. She knew I'd freak out if I ran into Wes like this, and she was trying to protect me. I didn't move fast enough, though. If I went to the office now, he'd see me. I had to go the other direction. I darted down the candy aisle and tried to blend in with the Jujubes, Kit Kat bars, and Reese's Peanut Butter Cups.

I texted Dhonielle. **Help. In candy aisle. Is coast clear?**

I waited, but there was no response. I wasn't sure what to do. I couldn't stand there forever. I stuck my head out of the aisle to peek. Big mistake. Wes had been looking my way. I quickly jumped back to where I had been. *Now what?* I couldn't stay there. I was like a sitting duck. I moved to the other side of the aisle and took a left. There was a huge cereal display. I just needed to hide behind it. I tried to wedge myself as best I could between the boxes and boxes of Honey Nut Cheerios and the shelves.

My phone buzzed. It was Dhonielle. **Candy aisle safe. Stay there. He's turning into aisle 9.**

NO! Aisle nine was *me*. This was not happening. Why didn't I listen to my mother? She would love to hear me say that. I tried to smooth down my hair, but I could feel the giant clumps. I couldn't even get my fingers through them. All right. If I couldn't fix the hair, maybe I could do something about the outfit. I pulled down the shirt, hoping I could tuck it in far enough to hide the hole, but the shirt was too small. There was no give. I loosened the drawstring on the pants and pulled them up higher. It covered the hole but also came up to my chest. I was pretty sure this looked worse. I was like the geeky dad in some old movie. I had to stop messing around. Wes was going to pass me any second. I needed to be still if there was any hope that he'd walk right by and miss me completely.

Don't breathe, Emily. Don't move a muscle. You are one with General Mills. You got this.

I closed my eyes and waited. *One Mississippi, two Mississippi, three Mississippi.* If I could just get to sixty Mississippi, I'd be in the clear. He'd be long gone by then. At about thirty Mississippi, I opened my eyes to sneak a look.

I wasn't alone.

"What are you doing?"

Wes was standing there waiting.

I had not expected to see him there. I hadn't expected to see *anyone* there. And when you think you're alone, and you open your eyes and there's a person directly in front of you, you jump back a bit. Which normally would not be a big deal. However, when you are crammed next to a cereal-box pyramid, bad things happen.

Dozens and dozens of boxes of Honey Nut Cheerios rained down on me. I kind of wanted to hide underneath them, but that really wasn't an option.

Wes's mouth dropped open. And a few nearby shoppers gasped. "Nothing to see here," I told them. "Continue shopping."

The loudspeaker went off again. It was Mark, another of my coworkers. "You're cleaning that up." I bet he and Dhonielle were gathered around the surveillance camera in the office watching me humiliate myself again.

I nodded. Restacking the boxes was the least of my problems. I started putting them back on their stand.

"Emily, what's going on?" Wes asked. He picked up some boxes and handed them to me.

"Was just looking for some cereal, and I slipped."

"What's *really* going on? Why were you hiding from me?"

"Hiding?" I scrunched up my face to try to show him I had no idea what he was talking about. "I wasn't hiding."

"I know you saw me."

I shook my head.

"Fine. Whatever you say." He turned to go.

"Wait." I forgot I was a horrible actress. Of course he saw through my lie. We'd been getting along so great, I didn't want to ruin it over something so stupid. "You were right. I was hiding from you."

He was waiting for an explanation, but I didn't have one. I couldn't say it was because I didn't want him to see me looking gross. That would just draw even more attention to the rat's nest on my head. *And* it might make him think that I liked him, and I couldn't have that unless I knew for sure that he liked me, too. I needed something else. Something that would make him stop questioning me.

"Tampons," I said.

"Huh?"

"I didn't want you to see me buying tampons. I thought it would make for weird conversation." Truthfully, I wouldn't

89

care if he saw me buying them. But I heard some guys get totally uncomfortable talking about that type of thing. I was hoping that he was one of them and that he'd drop the subject. But he was just looking at me like I made no sense, so I did the worst possible thing. I kept talking. "You know, tampons, maxi pads, tampons. Yep. Lots and lots of pads." *What was wrong with me?* If the items themselves didn't scare him away, then the weird girl who couldn't stop repeating the names of feminine-hygiene products should have. But he didn't seem fazed. I didn't know what to do. I had dug myself into a hole. I would have to up my game and go all-in. "You know, when it's that time of the month and all . . ." *Seriously, Emily. Shut up. Please, shut up. You have major issues.*

"You're not holding anything," he said.

"Huh?"

"You said you didn't want me to see you buying tampons, but you're not holding any—so there shouldn't have been a problem."

Were we really having this conversation? Why couldn't he act like an immature teenage guy just once? But no. He had to be all grown up and not even seem slightly uncomfortable talking about this. He was so freaking calm that he was catching everything. I felt like one of the guilty suspects on all those cop shows, who always get caught in their web of lies.

"When I saw you, I tossed it into the other aisle."

He stepped out and looked to the aisle to the left and to the right. "I don't see anything."

I started picking up more boxes of cereal. "I don't know. Maybe someone picked it up."

Right on cue, Dhonielle showed up, and I had never been

so happy to see someone in my whole life. She handed me a box of tampons. "First you throw things and then you knock down a display? Are you going for employee of the year?"

Relief washed over me. *Thank you, Dhonielle.* Her snooping saved me. I was so buying her the biggest, most awesome birthday present next month. "I'm sorry," I said. "I'm almost done cleaning up."

She smiled. "It's okay. Hi, Wes. I'll leave you two alone."

"See," I told him. "I wasn't lying."

"Good," he said, and piled on the last few boxes in the cereal pyramid. "I wouldn't want you to feel like you ever needed to run from me."

Run? I wanted to stay as close to him as possible, but I tried to act cool. I leaned back slightly, and, so much for cool, a cereal box fell and hit me on the head. "Ow."

"Careful," he said, picking the box back up. "You almost knocked the whole thing over again."

Why was I such a klutz? "Maybe you should be the one running from me," I told him. "First the play, and now knocking over a display in the grocery store. I'm an embarrassment."

"Emily, I don't care what some random strangers think. Or what happened in the scene. I thought it was funny. I told you that."

"So you're not totally mortified to be seen with me?" I asked.

"Not even a little. I'll prove it. I'll even give you a ride home."

"Yeah?"

"Yeah," he said.

Wes finished picking out a few groceries (he'd been on a

run for his mother, too), and I grabbed my carton of milk and took it and the box of tampons that I didn't really need at this point in time, but had no choice but to buy, to the checkout.

We walked out of the store, and I realized this is what I wanted: a guy who didn't care if I knocked down food displays or butchered Shakespeare or wore sweatpants up to my armpits. I wanted Wes, a guy who appreciated me for me.

16

Dhonielle was sitting on the bench in front of the grocery store. "Shouldn't you be working?" I joked as Wes and I passed by.

She shrugged. "I wanted to make sure you and all your mess were long gone before I went back in there." Then she explained to Wes the real reason. "I'm on my fifteen-minute break. I've been at work since six AM."

I really didn't know how she did these morning shifts all the time. I was always miserable after I did them, but I was much more of a night person than she was. "Seems like a rather boring break," I told her.

She shook her head as if in defeat. "Well, that's what happens when there's no one to play cart-lympics with."

"Cart-lympics?" Wes asked.

"Only the best sport in the world, created by yours truly," I informed him. "I know you're all into lacrosse, but I have to tell you, you're missing out. My game has yours beat."

"Is that so?"

"Absolutely. Right, Dhonielle?"

"I'd have to agree," she said.

"You don't have me sold," Wes said, clearly trying to hold back a smile, but I saw that dimple of his make an appearance. "Just how do you play cart-lympics?"

I shook my head. "We could tell you, but . . ."

"What? You'd have to kill me?"

"That's one way to go," I answered. "I was going to say it'd be a lot more fun to show you."

"You're on," he said, and gestured for me and Dhonielle to lead the way.

I knew I probably should have been heading home, but I really wanted to hang out. I looked at my sack with the milk. It was chilly enough out that it would be fine for a bit, and we were only going to play 'til Dhonielle's break was over. It wasn't like there was much of a risk of the milk spoiling, and I'd still get home in plenty of time to make the mac and cheese. It took less than an hour to prepare, and my parents' potluck wasn't until six PM. Besides, how could I resist introducing cart-lympics to more people?

It wasn't much of a choice. I had to stay.

We walked behind the store to the lot where the trucks dropped off the groceries. Dhonielle held out her hands and said, "Welcome to our course." Then she grabbed the shopping cart we kept back there, rolled it over to us, and jumped in.

I put both hands on the handle and in my best announcer voice declared, "Welcome to the cart-lympics, the death-defying, soon-to-be-world-renowned, Olympic-worthy grocery-cart races. The challenge, if you choose to accept it, is to make it around the course in the fastest possible time. First, you head north up the lot." I started pushing the cart. "When you hit the yield sign, circle four times. This takes skill. You want to get the best

94

time, but if you're too dizzy, you may mess up." Then I pushed Dhonielle back in the direction we came from. "Next you head south, making a quick left just before the grass, and then you must stop right at the white line. If you cross over, even an inch, your time is disqualified."

Wes started laughing. "And why is there a person in the cart?"

"For fun, of course," I told him.

"This doesn't seem too hard," he said.

"You say that now," Dhonielle warned him. "But after those spins, you sometimes wind up going the wrong direction. Not only does it cut your time, but you end up feeling more than a little loopy."

"That was the demo." I pulled out my phone, punched up the timer, and handed it to Dhonielle. "Now we mean business. Ready?"

Dhonielle nodded. "I'll count you down. Three, two, one, go!"

I raced my way up the lot, circled four times as Dhonielle kept track of each rotation, made my way back, and parked the cart like a pro.

"One minute, thirty-two seconds," she declared.

"Still champion," I cheered, and lapped around the cart doing my lame attempt at a Rocky impersonation. "My best was one minute, twenty-four."

"I'm next," Dhonielle said, and hopped out of the cart. "Wes, darling," she said in one of her theatrical voices. "Would you do me the honor of being my passenger? I promise I shall not get us killed." She assured him that we get a warning before any cars or trucks enter the area. A gate has to open before a vehicle can get into the lot. "And I've only crashed the cart into the sign or a wall once or twice."

"Or three or four times," I added. "But I'm still in one piece, so you should be okay."

"Don't listen to her. I'm a great cart driver."

"I'm in," he said, and hopped inside.

I held the timer this time and cheered as they made it to the yield sign. They headed back my way, and I almost doubled over laughing from the sight of Wes's expression. He looked more than a little panic-stricken. "A minute, fifty-nine seconds," I announced when they stopped. "You should have seen your face," I told him.

"You have no control in there. You feel like you're going to go flying off."

"It's like a roller-coaster ride," I said. "It's kind of exhilarating."

"But on a roller coaster, I'm not getting pushed by a person who's half-dizzy."

"I'd say full dizzy," Dhonielle chimed in.

"Even better," he said, getting out of the cart.

"You've got to trust that the person won't let go no matter what," she said.

I took Wes's spot in the cart. "Well, I trust you," I told him. "Ready?"

"You sure?" he asked.

"Yep." I didn't give him time to think about backing out. "Three, two, one, go!" Wes took off, and I started screaming woo-hoo as we made our way through the course. I loved the rush of the wind as we raced up and down. And the look of concentration on Wes's face as he circled the yield sign was an added bonus. He was taking my game seriously. I kind of loved that.

He was extracareful pulling up to the line, making sure he didn't go over. It cost him some seconds, but he parked perfectly. "Two minutes and fifty-two seconds," I said. "Impressive. That's the best first-time score yet."

Wes looked proud of himself. "Yeah?"

"Mine was three minutes, twenty seconds," I admitted.

"And I was four minutes even," Dhonielle said. She looked at her phone. "I hate to break up the party, but my break is over. I need to get back in."

We said good-bye to her, and then I turned back to Wes. "One more round?"

"Definitely." He put his hands on the handle and stared right into my eyes. "Get ready to have your record crushed."

I raised an eyebrow at him. "Big talk from a newbie. Let's see what you got."

I kept my eyes glued on his, and as I yelled "go," Wes and I took off together.

When we finally came to a stop, my heart was racing, but I knew it had nothing to do with the game.

17

"Are you going to be able to drive?" I asked Wes as we got to his car.

"Yeah, but we may need to sit for a few minutes first."

He was a little wobbly from cart-lympics. After Dhonielle went inside, Wes and I took a few more turns. Three inside the cart and three as the runner each. I don't think either of our equilibriums were entirely back on track.

"That's some game you created," he said, his cheeks still rosy from the adrenaline rush and his hair almost as messy as mine. "One of these days, I will beat you."

"I don't know. I am the champ, after all. But I will take that as a challenge."

"You're on. You'll have to let me know when you're working."

He was the first non–Northside Grocery person I'd introduced to my game. Not even Kayla or Jill had played. And it was cool that he seemed into it. The idea of his coming to visit me during my work breaks made me shiver—in the good way. I couldn't help but wonder if maybe he wanted more than friendship. I mean, my heart told me we were supposed to be together. And I was pretty sure he sensed it, too.

I'd played cart-lympics with Dhonielle and nearly everyone who worked at the grocery store who was under twenty-two years old, but never did I get the sense that they were looking at me the way Wes looked at me after we hit the finish line. There just seemed to be this invisible force that radiated between us. And it didn't feel like just my imagination.

I had grabbed my bike, and Wes was putting it on the rack on the back of his car. It wasn't the one he usually drove. "Another new car?" I asked.

"My dad's," he said. "He likes me to take it every so often, so I don't forget how to drive a stick shift."

He opened the passenger door for me and waited until I was fully inside before he closed it. It was supersweet. I loved that he always did that. My dad did that for my mom, and while Dhonielle said things like that were corny and women can get their own doors and don't need a man to do it, I liked it. It didn't mean I wasn't capable, it just meant he was being extracourteous to me. The same way I was trying to be to him by leaning over to his side of the car and unlocking his door. Sure, it was a small gesture, but I think the world could use more people doing kind things for one another, even if it is something tiny. And, hey, if the person going out of the way for me is also somebody I find incredibly cute, then that's just an added bonus.

When Wes got in the car, he didn't seem to be in too big of a rush to get going. He sat back and ran his hands through his hair, which was completely windblown. It looked hot. It reminded me what a mess I knew I looked like. Yet somehow being around Wes, I didn't feel like a disaster. I actually felt good.

I glanced at the clock. I'd been gone for about an hour. If I didn't get home soon, my mother would probably send out a search party, but I didn't want to rush my moment with Wes, either.

"How often do you work here?" he asked.

"Just two or three shifts a week during the school year," I said. "Some combination of Friday, Saturday, or Sunday and the occasional weeknight; but over breaks and the summer, I'm here a lot more."

"Must be hard to fit it into your schedule," he said.

I smiled at him. "Well, I don't play a sport and sign up for every activity in existence like some people in this car." I also had a nonexistent dating life, but I decided not to mention that.

"You do other stuff. You helped put together the dance."

"Not by choice." I almost threw in a dig about Amanda, but I bit my tongue. He was still friendly with her, and I didn't want to ruin the mood by being all negative.

"Maybe not, but you still did it. It looks like it will be fun."

Why was he bringing up the dance? Was this his way of hinting that he wanted to go with me? Was he waiting for me to ask him? "I'm looking forward to it," I said, chickening out from asking what I really wanted to know.

I looked away from him and down at my lap.

His eyes must have followed mine, because he said, "Oh, I better get you home before your groceries are out too long."

"Thanks," I said, but I was secretly kicking myself. I hadn't meant to stare at the sack of milk and make him think I wanted to leave. I just got nervous looking at him.

I watched as he put his hand on the stick shift.

"Have you ever driven a manual car?" he asked.

I shook my head. "I have no clue how it works."

"It's not too hard once you get the hang of it. Here, I'll show you. Give me your hand."

He didn't have to ask me twice. I put out my hand; he took it and put it on the stick shift, and put his hand on top of mine.

I was fairly sure I was going to explode from giddiness right there. He started saying something about holding down the clutch with his left foot and doing something else with his right foot, but honestly I wasn't sure what he was saying. All I could think about was that WES ROSENTHAL'S hand was on top of mine.

What was happening?! This was so strange.

Did he really want to teach me about driving a stick shift, or was this his sly way of getting close to me? *Why couldn't I read him?* It had to be a flirty thing, didn't it? I couldn't imagine Wes doing this with Omar or Mason. But what did I know?

"To get the car into first gear," he said, guiding my hand up and to the left, "we move the stick this way."

I nodded but kept my eyes on our hands. I was sure I was blushing. Not just because he was practically holding my hand, but because the whole thing was surreal. And the immature, childish part of me couldn't help but think of the sexual innuendos surrounding his teaching me how to hold his stick. Was he oblivious to it? He really was a lot more mature than I was, but I knew two people who weren't. Kayla and Jill were going to have a field day with this one when I told them.

The car started moving. Wes was talking more gibberish about easing off the clutch and giving the car gas. Then he guided my hand downward. "We pull down from first into second gear like this."

"Nice," I said, because I felt I should say something.

"Just keep your hand there."

I had no intention of moving it.

"When we stop, we move it to neutral." He moved my hand again when we came to a red light. And quite frankly, I have no recollection of what he said after that. The rest of the ride home, the only thing I could make sense of was my feelings. I was totally, head over heels, crazy for Wes.

His hand stayed on top of mine until we reached my house. It even lingered there for a few seconds after he stopped the car. *This had to mean something.* You didn't do this with someone who was just your friend.

When we got out of the car, he took my bike off the rack. We stood across from each other. The only thing separating us was the bike. He had one hand on the handlebars and the other on the seat. I mirrored his position.

This time, I made sure to look right at him when I spoke. "Thanks a lot for the ride." My voice was lower and breathier than usual. I think it was because I was having a hard time keeping my heartbeat under control.

"Anytime," he said. He didn't make a move to leave.

Was he going to kiss me?

Neither of us spoke, we just stood there. My breath was getting shallower and shallower. *Come on, Wes. Please make a move.*

Ten seconds passed. Fifteen. We were just standing there, looking at each other. He had to feel what I was feeling.

I moved my fingers on the bike seat a little closer to his. I was pretty sure his edged forward ever so slightly, too. It was my turn. I moved my hand forward a little more, and he did the same, but he stopped shy of touching me. *Should I just put my hand on his?* Yes, that's what I needed to do. I needed to be bold. I just needed to get up the courage.

Do it, do it, do it, do it, do it, do it, I cheered myself on. Only, I chickened out. But I let my fingers brush his slightly. It was enough, he leaned in. WES ROSENTHAL WAS GOING TO KISS ME. Only, he didn't get the chance. We were interrupted.

By my father.

"Emily," he called out from the window of his car as he pulled into the driveway.

NO! He was ruining my moment. He couldn't have come home five minutes later? I turned to my dad. "I'll be in in a minute," I said, and watched him go inside.

I quickly looked back at Wes, but the spell was broken. He wasn't going to kiss me, not now, not with the threat of my father looking out and seeing us. "I should probably get going," he said.

"Yeah," I said, "and I better get inside. The milk and all. I have macaroni and cheese to make. It's really good. You should try it. Well, not today, but sometime maybe. Okay, bye."

I was so flustered that I ran toward my house. WITHOUT MY BIKE. I had left Wes standing there holding it. I only realized it when I got to my door, so I had to run all the way back. "Ha-ha," I said, taking my bike from him. "Almost forgot this. Wouldn't want to do that. Well, thanks again. Have fun getting home. You know what I mean." He probably didn't, but that was okay. Because I was fairly confident that Wes liked me. Liked me liked me. Babbling and all.

18

I felt like Snow White as I danced around the kitchen making the mac and cheese. I was practically floating I was so happy. I had found my prince. I couldn't wait to look into those amazing eyes again. And I didn't have to! I had social media.

I ran upstairs, got comfy on my bed, popped open my computer, and went onto his GroupIt page. I loved his profile picture. It was one of him midlaugh. He had that perfect, makes-you-smile-when-you-hear-it laugh, too. He really was amazing. I could spend all day just looking at his photos. There were a lot, too. A whole page of Wes. Thank you, Internet.

So many people posted pictures and videos from the other day to his page. I clicked on a clip of Wes trying to catch me during our Shakespeare scene. He managed to look good even under crazy circumstances. And how sweet was he, trying to make sure I didn't fall? I hoped I didn't hurt him. He didn't look as if he was in pain. I couldn't help but watch the video loop over and over and over again. We actually looked pretty cute together.

But not all of the new tagged photos included me. There was, uck, one with Amanda at the hospital. I guess I had no right to be upset that he went to visit her, but I didn't have to like it. Or the fact that they looked happy. Too happy. And the picture had 149 likes and thirty-five comments. Most of them saying how great they looked.

None of that matters, Emily. Wes likes you. He almost kissed you!!! I chose to ignore the Amanda photo and clicked over to some older, less offensive ones. Wes looked good in every single picture. I don't think he knew how to take a bad photo. That could have had something to do with his being the best-looking guy at Shaker Heights High. Sure, Amanda's ex, Cody, was close. He was that whole Abercrombie & Fitch generic hot, but there was just something about Wes.

I clicked on an album from his family's trip to Disney World. It was him, his parents, and his brother, and they were all wearing Mickey Mouse ears. They looked goofy and fun. And totally adorable. I tapped over to his brother's page. I'd seen all of Wes's pics before, maybe his brother would have some hidden gems.

Neal had the same eyes as Wes. It was nice seeing them together. I kept clicking through his albums. There was one of them celebrating their dad's birthday. Another with their dog in the park. Some of Neal alone on a bike path. I wondered if Wes took those photos.

My computer froze as I tried to move to the next picture. "Come on," I whispered to the screen and started tapping my mouse like a madwoman. I hated when this happened. Instead of a car, I probably needed a new laptop. I hit the power button. And as it asked me if I was sure I wanted to power off, my Internet started running again, so I hit no. A bunch of screens raced past. All that clicking I had done was going through. It was as if GroupIt had a mind of its own. Pictures of Neal at a race, playing chess, and doing who knows what were moving at warp speed. I tried to stop it. I tried to go to my profile page. But it wasn't listening to my commands. Instead, crazy things started happening. **Do you want to tag Emily Stein in this photo?** popped up. NO! I did NOT want to tag myself in one of Wes's brother's photos. What had I hit? I tried to click no, I tried to stop it, but the screen just passed me by. *Why wouldn't it go back?* Why wasn't it working? *Did it do it?* Did it *tag* me? Why wouldn't the stupid machine behave? I powered it off and grabbed my phone.

My heart was racing as I logged on to Neal's GroupIt page. *It's going to be fine. Nothing happened. You didn't tag yourself.* Yet my reassurances weren't calming me down. I still had that nagging feeling as I clicked through his photos. So far, so good. There was no sign of me yet. My breathing was returning to normal. Then it happened. A new notification message popped up. **Neal Rosenthal commented on a photo you are tagged in.**

I closed my eyes. Maybe this was a dream. A bad nightmare that I'd wake up from. But when I looked back at my phone, I knew that wasn't the case. This was *really* happening. The notification would take me straight to the picture, but did I really want to see it? My finger shook as I decided whether to press the screen.

I didn't want to, but I had to know for sure.

I went for it.

No, no, no, no, no, no, noooooooooooo. I threw my phone down on the bed.

It was worse than I could have imagined.

I stared at the spot where the phone had landed. It was like a nuclear bomb that was ready to blow up my life. The picture I had tagged myself in wasn't just a regular picture of Neal. (Of course not. Why would my life be that easy?) Instead, it was a picture of Neal holding his hands in a heart shape. A picture that now had my name smack on top of it.

19

I got my mom to give me a ride to school the next morning. I had to get there early to see Wes. I needed to explain about the picture. He'd understand once I told him the story. He had to. He knew I was prone to doing stupid things. But what if he thought it was weird I was looking at his brother's GroupIt page? I really topped myself this time. It was one thing to overcome the Shakespeare scene from hell, but tagging yourself in your crush's brother's picture? That was a whole other ballpark. It was like announcing to the world that I had been spying on him. As if I was some cyberstalker. *Just relax*, I told myself. It was going to be fine. Wes wasn't going to care. At least I hoped not.

Only, I didn't get a chance to find out. Wes didn't show up at his locker. Ever since he started driving, it was about fifty-fifty whether he made it to school on time. I would have to try back again before I went to study hall. He usually dropped off his stuff then. Yeah, okay, I may have memorized his schedule. So much for avoiding stalker status.

When I went back later, he was there, as suspected. But he wasn't alone. His brother was with him. I definitely wasn't approaching Wes with Neal standing there—not to talk about the photo. I had to wait for him to leave. So I stayed hidden around the corner. I couldn't help but spy.

"Someone called you *what*?" Wes asked. "Who was it?"

"It doesn't matter," Neal said. He looked upset. They both did.

"It matters to me." I had never seen Wes look so intense.

"Forget I said anything."

"I'm not going to forget it." Wes put his hands on his brother's shoulders. "If *anyone* gives you a hard time, you come to me, you hear me? And I know you keep saying you don't want to sit with me at lunch, but I don't care. Enough with spending the period in the computer lab. You're sitting with me today and from now on. Let someone even try to say something to you with me there."

Neal nodded, but you could see his whole demeanor change. He seemed to lighten up. Wes was a really good brother. I loved the way he was always there for his family. It couldn't have been easy for Neal to be a kid genius, but being his brother had to have its challenges, too, and if Wes got jealous or annoyed, he never showed it. In fact, if anything, he was proud and overprotective.

I snuck away. Now definitely wasn't the time to talk to Wes. He had other things to worry about than my tagging some photo. I'd catch him around lunchtime.

"Where have you been?" Jill asked me as I walked into study hall.

"Trying to talk to Wes," I said.

"And?" she questioned.

I shook my head as we headed to our seats. "No luck. I can't get him alone, and I'm afraid the longer I wait, the worse it's going to be."

"I really think you are getting worked up over nothing. He probably didn't even see it. Normal people don't study their little brother's social media pages."

"Maybe . . ."

"Seriously," she said, "I don't even remember the last time I looked at my sister's old pictures. I bet you're fine." She pulled out a lipstick and a compact mirror.

"Lipstick?" I questioned. Jill rarely bothered with things like makeup.

"Was just in the mood."

"Really? And it has nothing to do with lover boy?" I wiggled my eyebrows at her.

"Okay, fine, maybe," she blurted out and glanced at the door expectantly. "I haven't seen him yet. And with the break, it's been a full week."

The bell rang, and there was still no sign of Seth Werner. Jill got one of her I-am-in-panic-mode looks. That was the thing with her. You always knew exactly what she was thinking. Her face was easy to read. If only I had been able to figure out Wes like that, my life would have been a whole lot simpler right now.

"I'm sure he'll show," I said. "I saw him in first period. He's here." I definitely understood what it was like to be anxious to see someone. And Jill had it bad for Seth. He was tall, lanky, with a nose a little too big for his face, yet still kind of hot. Ever since he sat next to her in study hall a few weeks ago, and she saw him reading a book not assigned by a teacher, she was smitten. A cute guy who likes to read is, like, a major turn-on for Jill.

"You guys would make a great couple. You know that, right?"

She swatted my arm. "Shhhhh."

I wasn't about to drop the subject. This was the perfect distraction. Not only did I get to think about something other than my failures, but it would also help my best friend—whom I seriously owed. "You should just ask him out," I said. "He clearly likes you. Watching you two is gag-worthy."

"You mean like you and Wes at rehearsals? I didn't see you asking him out."

I started doodling in my notebook. "It's not the same."

"Oh, please," she said.

"Fine," I relented. "Maybe it was. But I highly doubt you want to be like me. Make a total fool of yourself, almost kiss him, then tag yourself in his brother's picture—and still no date."

"So why don't you take your own advice and ask him?"

The conversation was tabled as Seth ran into class. He waved a hall pass at the teacher and bounded into the seat on the other side of Jill.

"I was at the library," he said, holding up some worn-out paperback. "You said you liked mysteries, so I signed this one out for you. I read it last year, and it was amazing. You'll never guess who the killer is. Okay, I can't tell you anything more or I'll ruin it for you. You have to read it, and then we can talk about it."

He was talking so fast I could barely keep up, but Jill was

beaming. Whether he knew it or not, Seth had found the way to her heart. For Jill, getting a handpicked book specially for her was better than receiving three dozen roses. I had a feeling he wouldn't have to wait long to discuss the book with her. It was a fairly safe bet that Jill would have the whole thing finished before she went to bed.

Seth handed it to her, his fingers lightly swiping hers. His cheeks turned a light shade of pink. And so did hers. It was actually cute. Well, for me to watch. It was probably pretty embarrassing for them. I'd seen Jill have crushes before, but never like this. She looked frozen, as if she forgot how to form a sentence. And Jill was *never* at a loss for words. "Thanks," she finally squeaked out.

"Sure." He looked away. "Just thought you'd like it." He was clearly having insecurity issues, too. With their rate of shyness, they'd be lucky if they went on their first date by the time they graduated college.

"Ask him out," I mumbled so that only she would hear.

"Shut up," she hissed back.

"What?" Seth asked.

The look she gave me was a mixture of pure terror mixed with I-want-to-tape-your-mouth-shut-for-eternity. "Nothing," she said.

She was probably going to kill me now but thank me later, because like it or not I was going to help her romance along. "I was asking her about the dance." I pulled a flyer out of my bag. I still had a bunch from when Amanda made me pass them out. "It's Friday. I helped organize it, and I want Jill to go. Maybe you can help me convince her?"

Jill dug her heel into my foot, but I wasn't one to let a little pain stop me. My love life was a question mark, but that didn't mean my friend couldn't wind up with the guy of her dreams.

"I've never been to one of the dances," Seth said.

"Really?" Jill asked.

He shrugged. "I'm not a great dancer."

"That's not a problem," I butted in. "Jill can teach you. She's awesome."

"Yeah?" he asked.

"I wouldn't say awesome," she answered, and this time it was my turn to kick her. She had the perfect opening and was blowing it. "But . . ." she snapped out of her stupor. "I'm okay. I'd definitely show you. If you wanted."

Seth stole a glance at her. "It could be fun. Sure."

"Cool," she said, sneaking a look back.

"Great, it's a date," I chimed in so there would be no confusion later on.

Jill stomped on my foot extrahard this time, but I knew she was happy. Not only did I help snag her a date to the dance, but I also saved her countless hours of wondering if they were going as friends, dance teacher/dance student, or as a couple.

I was tempted to butt in some more, but I didn't think my foot could handle another Jill hit, so I left them alone and went back to obsessing over my own problem. What was Wes going to think about my tagging his brother? I hated GroupIt. Why hadn't I been faster to log back on? If only I had taken the tag off the photo before Neal commented. I cringed when I thought about what he wrote. *Cool, Emily, I like older women.* Then he threw in a winky face. My name was now emblazoned for posterity under his picture. I thought about messaging him to take it down. But it didn't really matter. Either way, he was bound to tell his brother. Neal didn't know me; our only real connection was Wes. If he was as smart as everyone said he was, he'd definitely put two and two together. So there was basically no getting around it. I had to own up to everything. Lunch couldn't come fast enough.

After class, Jill held me back. "What was that?"

"My paying back my best friend. I told you I'd make it up to you."

"And did you ever." A huge smile spread over her face. "I just got a date with Seth. I think I'm in shock. Over-the-moon, ecstatic shock. Now we just have to get things right with you and Wes."

"I know," I said, and I linked arms with her. "And I had a lot of time to think while you and Seth were busy swooning over each other. I know what I'm going to do. I'm just going to fess up that I was looking at his brother's pics because I wanted to know more about his family, because I like him. Then I'm going to do it."

"Do what?"

"Ask him to the dance."

I, Emily Stein, was about to pour my heart out to Wes Rosenthal and pray he didn't break it.

20

When the bell rang for lunch, I booked it back to Wes's locker.

I was nearly out of breath by the time I reached him. I really needed more exercise than the occasional game of cart-lympics.

"Hey," he said, and gave me a big smile.

"Hey," I answered. He seemed happy to see me, but that meant he probably didn't know about the picture. I had to get it over with. Rip off the Band-Aid. "I have a confession. I did something stupid. Again."

He raised an eyebrow. I scrunched my eyes closed and kept going, letting the words run from my mouth. "I was looking at all the pictures we were tagged in from the scene and somehow I wound up on your brother's page and my computer got a mind of its own and I tagged myself in one of his pictures. It was an accident." Okay, I may have veered slightly from my plan to disclose *everything*, like how I was spying because of my massive crush, but it was scary to be that open.

"Yeah, Neal showed me that last night. I figured it was some sort of mistake."

I opened my eyes back up. Was he serious? Did he really not think it was a big deal?

"One time," he said, "I accidentally clicked 'love' on a post where my uncle announced he and my aunt were getting a divorce. I didn't even realize I did it until my mom said something. My finger must have touched it while I was swiping on my phone. Who knows what else I accidentally liked? Dogfighting rings? End-of-the-world theories? Crazy political posts? I swear if that has happened, it wasn't me, just my fat fingers."

Once again, Wes had managed to turn around an embarrassing situation and made me smile. I wanted to go to the dance with him now more than ever. I wasn't going to have a repeat of his bar mitzvah. This time, I was asking him to be my date.

"Did you hit 'like' for the dance?" I asked. "I was thinking it would be fun, and I was . . ." *Spit it out, Emily!* "wondering if you had plans?"

Wes shifted on his feet and looked kind of awkward. Before he could answer, Amanda shimmied up and slid under his arm. "He's going with me."

What?!

This couldn't be happening. It felt as if my blood had stopped flowing and an invisible force had managed to thrust a hand all the way to my heart and ripped it out. I might have looked normal on the outside, but on the inside I was hollow.

He. Was. Going. To. The. Dance. With. Amanda.

How was this possible? Just yesterday Wes had almost kissed me. Had I read it all wrong? I couldn't even think straight.

"You weren't trying to ask Wes out, were you?" Amanda

asked, and gave a haughty little laugh like the idea was so out-landish. I hated her. First day back to school after days in the hospital, and she couldn't even pretend to be nice? "You know," she continued, "I thought you were into Neal, at least accord-ing to GroupIt. Maybe you could ask him out instead."

I thought I was going to throw up or pass out or something. Now would have been a great time for the floor to open up and swallow me.

"Amanda," Wes started to say.

But I didn't need him fighting my battles. He was no better than she was. Sure, she was rubbing my nose in the fact that he didn't like me. But *he* was the one who led me on. I looked down the hall. Jill and Kayla were standing there. I decided to pull strength from them. Wes didn't want me? Fine. He needed to know that I didn't want him, either, and that I never had. I could pull that off. *Maybe*.

"It's okay," I told him. "It's not like I was asking you out anyway," I said with a laugh. "I mean, come on. We're just really good friends. I don't look at you like that." I grimaced for extra effect.

"Uh-huh," Amanda said, her voice all smug.

I was not going to let her win. Not this time. "Kayla, Jill, and I are all going as friends. And since Wes wasn't dating any-one, I thought maybe he'd want to join us," I informed Amanda. "He *is* good friends with Kayla's boyfriend. It just made sense. And he's been a really good *friend* to me. That's all." Oh, God. It was starting. The babbling. "I mean, he gave me rides home from rehearsal and things, so I figured if he wanted to join and not go alone, he should. That's what friends do for each other."

How many times was I going to use the word friends? "But obviously, if he's going with you, that won't be necessary."

"You're going in a group?" she asked. "You know it's a semiformal, right?"

Of course I knew. I had to make all the stupid signs. "Yeah," I said. "So what? The more people, the more fun."

Amanda tilted her head slightly and looked at me as if I were an alien creature from another planet who didn't speak her language. "Semiformal means a lot of slow songs, and you'll have a much better time with a date. If you can get one, that is."

"I'm sure it will be fun either way," Wes added.

Oh, shut up, Wes.

"I'm not worried," I told her.

She shrugged. "Well, I guess you're used to embarrassing situations. I watched the *Romeo and Juliet* scene when I was in the hospital. It was priceless. The doctor had to take away my iPad, I was laughing so hard. She was afraid I would pop a stitch." It looked as if Wes was going to say something again, but Amanda kept talking. "Did Wes tell you? I begged Mrs. Heller, and she's going to let me do the scene again next week when I'm up for it. She's even going to let all the juniors come watch. I guess she wants them to see how the scene really should be performed."

"Well, good for you," I said.

Amanda was getting everything she wanted, and I was getting my heart broken. I couldn't be around them anymore. I didn't want them to see how hurt I was.

"I should get going," I said. "Kayla and Jill are waiting for me. Have fun at the dance." *I hadn't meant to say that.* "I'm sure

I'll see you before then, though. Since today is just Monday. But whatever. You get the point. See ya later."

Then I turned on my heels and walked away from the new power couple so they wouldn't be able to see the tears that were about to come streaming down my face.

21

Kayla, Jill, and I skipped the cafeteria and went to the bathroom by the music room for an emergency how-could-this-be-happening-am-I-just-having-a-horrible-nightmare conversation.

Aside from us, the lavatory was empty. After Jill double-checked under the stalls and grabbed me some toilet paper to dry my eyes, we all sat down. Me with my back to the door so no one would be able to come in, and them across from me. I kept reliving the horror show in my head. *He's going with me.* Amanda's words played over and over.

I filled my friends in on everything that had happened. As I spoke, my eyes started to water, which turned into a full-on sobfest, and they both raced over to put an arm around me. I didn't hold back. This was the worst day ever. And now I would have to face Wes in English. How was I supposed to smile, say hello, act as if everything was cool and that we were friends when he just crushed my heart?

"Em, I'm so sorry," Jill said.

Kayla nodded in agreement.

"I just don't get it," I said. I was sure Wes was feeling the same way I was. The way he looked at me after cart-lympics, the driving lesson, that moment in front of my house. I know I didn't make all that up. I wiped away my tears. "He seemed so into me yesterday. How could he have almost kissed me when he was going to the dance with Amanda?"

"I don't know. Maybe he just realized how strong his feelings were for you, and he was planning to cancel on Amanda and ask you to the dance instead?" Jill offered.

"I doubt it. And even so, that still meant he chose her first. I just don't understand why he would be like that with me if he wanted her? Was he just playing me?"

"It might be something else," Kayla said. "Maybe—"

"No." I shook my head. "Don't make excuses for him. It is what it is, and I don't need someone like him anyway. It's better that I try to get over it and move on."

"On the upside," Jill said, "you handled it really, really well."

"Yeah," Kayla agreed. "Now at least he thinks you weren't into him, either. And from where we were standing, you looked really calm and collected."

I guess that was something. "Thanks. I just want to not even think about it anymore."

My stomach growled. Kayla dug into her lunch sack and pulled out a turkey sandwich and gave me half. Maybe food would take my mind off things.

"You guys are not eating that in here, are you?" Jill made a gagging sound and scrunched up her face as Kayla took a giant bite.

"What? We're hungry. It's lunchtime." At least that's what I think she said. Her mouth was full, and her words were hard to make out.

Jill stared at Kayla in mock disgust. They were trying to make me smile, and it was semiworking.

"You should make . . ." Then a bunch of words came out of Kayla's food-filled mouth that I couldn't translate.

"What?"

Jill stepped in. "I think what she's trying to say is that you should make him regret his decision."

"Me? How would I pull that off?" It sounded kind of crazy, but I had to admit the idea made me feel a little better. I picked at the sandwich.

The door behind me started to inch forward, and I leaned back against it with all my body weight. "It's out of order," I yelled, taking all my anger at Wes and the situation out on the stranger.

The person kept pushing.

I fought back. "I said it's broken. Try the one down the hall."

She must have left, and I relaxed against the door.

Kayla tossed me a couple of mini candy bars. "Here, chocolate makes everything feel better."

"I doubt it." But I unwrapped it and tossed it into my mouth just the same. "So how am I going to make him regret it?" I asked.

"Simple, you have fun, smile, show him how amazing your life is without him. He'll totally miss hanging out with you. Everyone knows you are way better than Amanda. And in the meantime, maybe we can even find you an amazing new guy."

"That's it." Jill clapped her hands together. "I always get over an old crush when I find a new one."

"I don't want anyone new."

"But you want to be over Wes, don't you?" Kayla said. "Jace has a lot of friends. I could totally hook you up."

"Wes is his friend," I informed her.

"And for the past three years you wouldn't let me get Jace involved with that or even tell him you liked Wes. But he has a lot of other friends. Let me see what I can do."

"Hey," Jill said. "You never tried to set me up."

"Because you think all his friends are idiots." Kayla tossed a piece of candy at her. "Which they aren't."

"I don't think they're idiots. I just think they are a little self-absorbed."

"Speaking of self-absorbed, can we get back to talking about me, please?!" I grabbed the candy that Kayla had thrown at Jill and ate it.

"That was mine," she said.

"You wouldn't have eaten it in here anyway," Kayla told her, and tossed her another one. "But, yes, let's get back to you, Em. The way I see it, you have a few choices. You can try to get over it, talk to him, and be friends again. You can ignore him. You can make him wish he hadn't been so stupid. Or you can move on."

"Well, I'm definitely not trying to talk to him again. And I have no choice but to move on. He already asked Amanda out. I need to be over him." I closed my eyes. *You're over Wes Rosenthal. You're over Wes Rosenthal.* I wondered how many times I needed to say that to make it stick.

"So you're completely done with him?" Jill asked.

I played back again everything that had happened. The moment I asked him if he had plans for the dance kept nipping at my brain. That look of panic on his face. He knew perfectly well how Amanda had treated me the past few months and how she acted toward everyone, and yet he still asked her out. Of all the people in school, he picked her. And then he made it seem as if he wanted me. That wasn't a friend. The more I thought about it, the angrier I got. I wasn't going to be one of those girls who pined over someone she couldn't have. Especially someone who acted like a creep. He wanted Amanda—he could have her. I was so done with Wes Rosenthal.

22

My one and only class with Wes was last period—English. There wasn't assigned seating, but we basically all sat in the same spots we took on day one. For me, that was the back right corner next to Wes.

Well, today I was going to be a model student. Ryan Watkins would have to find a new seat, because I was taking his. Front row, right dab in the center. No one would bother me there.

"I guess someone's trying to kiss butt to make up for their star performance," Ryan said, dropping his stuff on his—scratch that—my desk. "Now get out of my seat."

"Clearly, I need to work on my English grade," I told him. "You do so well up here, I thought I'd take a lesson."

"Get out, Emily."

He was getting very worked up over a stupid seat, but I wasn't going to let him boss me around. Not today.

I pushed his stuff to the corner of my desk. "Guess you should have gotten here earlier."

"You're so annoying," he grumbled, but he took his things and moved to the desk next to me.

"See, was that so bad?" I asked him. "And now you get to spend the whole class next to yours truly."

"Lucky me."

I winked at him, and he rolled his eyes.

It felt weird being in the front. Everyone looked at me when they walked in. They weren't used to seeing me there. I was the one who tried to stay as far out of Mrs. Heller's line of vision as possible, but I still managed to get yelled at for talking every day. That's what happened when you sat next to your crush— you wound up chatting whenever you saw the opportunity. I certainly wasn't going to have that problem next to Ryan. My eyes were glued on the door as everyone filed in, but I quickly looked down at my book when I saw Wes.

I wondered if he was disappointed that I wasn't sitting by him, but then I reminded myself that I didn't care. I was done with him.

"Em," he called out. And while I technically knew it was impossible for my heart to stop beating while I was clearly still living and breathing, that's what it felt like. Why couldn't Wes just let me grieve in peace? He made his choice. He didn't want me, and I didn't need to make small talk with him. I quickly turned around to chat up the person behind me.

As luck would have it, it was Cody Burns. Handsome, popular, athletic Cody, who also happened to be Amanda's old boyfriend.

"Did we have homework?" I asked, and flashed him an extrabig smile. Yes, the flirtiness may have been for Wes's benefit, but this was a golden opportunity. If Wes could have picture-perfect Amanda, then I wanted him to think I could have her equally gorgeous ex. This way he'd know I wasn't lying when I said I wasn't into him.

"Nah, she gave us a break for the vacation."

"That's a relief." I didn't really have anything else to say to him. It wasn't as if we had a lot in common, but I had to keep the conversation going. "Do anything fun while we were off?"

"The usual. But"—he got a cocky grin—"I did see a few videos on GroupIt."

"Let me guess," I said. "I was the star."

"That you were. I missed the live performance. I decided ten points wasn't worth sitting through that much Shakespeare, but I heard your scene was worth watching. You didn't disappoint."

I should have known there was no escaping my online presence. I laughed like Cody had said something superfunny, because I could feel Wes still standing there.

"Heller make you move up here because of all that?" Cody asked, then he leaned forward on his desk. "Or did you just want to be closer to me?"

I'd forgotten how much of a flirt Cody could be, but today it was much appreciated. "Can't it be both?" I practically cooed.

Out of my peripheral vision, I saw Wes walk away. I felt a mixture of relief and disappointment.

The bell rang, and I turned from Cody and back to the front of the class, but I was having a hard time focusing. While I might have been away from Wes physically, he still hogged all my attention, and it was royally bugging me. He didn't deserve my headspace.

"Okay," Mrs. Heller said. "Now that we're done reading

A Midsummer Night's Dream, before we move on from Shakespeare, I thought it might be fun to look at some of his popular scenes. We got to see a portion of them during Shakespeare in the Heights Night, which I might add you all did an amazing job with."

Ryan looked right at me. "Almost all-est of us," he whispered loud enough for everyone to hear.

The class started to laugh.

My day was bad enough. I was not going to let him embarrass me, too. It was time for flirty, confident, funny Emily to make a very public appearance. I stood up, made sure to make eye contact with as many people as I could (except for Wes of course), and then I took a very elaborate bow. As everyone started applauding, I did three little curtsies. I got a few cheers and whistles, so I kept going, feeding off the class's energy. Throwing kisses, raising my arms in a victory sign, and so forth until Mrs. Heller cut me off.

"All right, all right," she said. "Some scenes may have gone a little smoother than others."

"Obviously, you're talking about mine," I said. "I think it was A-plus-worthy." And then I winked at Cody. Wes wasn't the only one who could throw them around like candy.

"Let's get back on track," Mrs. Heller said. Although I had to admit, I was kind of enjoying my class-clown status. It was a lot more fun when people were laughing with you instead of at you.

"As I was saying," she said, "there were many scenes and monologues we didn't get to. So today we're going to go over snippets of a few of them. For the first one, I'm going to need two volunteers."

Maybe it was the residual high from all the applause or just a short bout of stupidity, but before I knew it, my hand shot up in the air, and I announced, "I'll do-eth it."

"Haven't you killed Shakespeare enough?" Ryan asked.

"I can't be any worse," I told him.

"I wouldn't count on it," he said.

"Okay." Mrs. Heller cut him off before he could continue his insults. "Emily, come on up. The first passage we're doing is from act 2, scene 1 of *The Taming of the Shrew*."

"Typecasting," Ryan mumbled.

I chose to ignore him.

"I need a Petruchio to join our Katharina . . . our Kate," Mrs. Heller said.

Wes stood up. "I guess I should do it."

Was it too late to back out? I didn't want to be up there with him. Did he really have to volunteer? Getting over him was going to be a lot harder if he kept popping up everywhere. He needed to leave me alone. He owed me that much at least.

"Why you?" Ryan asked. "You think you can tame her?"

"What? No." Wes looked shaken. "I didn't mean it like that at all. I just meant because we did the last scene together. This is like a second chance."

What was he trying to prove? Wasn't it bad enough he led me on? Now he wanted to cash in on this scene, too? This was supposed to be my moment to show people I'm over the *Romeo and Juliet* fiasco. I certainly didn't want Wes by my side. Not after what he just put me through.

"This play," Mrs. Heller said, oblivious to my obvious discomfort, "is controversial. Many say it has numerous misogynistic elements. Kate is a feisty woman who knows what she wants. And Petruchio here thinks he can get her to be an obedient bride. When they meet, they exchange some rapid-fire banter that gets a little down and dirty."

"Nice," Cody said, and a few of the guys snickered.

"Settle down," Mrs. Heller said, and handed out some printed pages to Wes and me. "I marked where to start."

Ryan pulled out his phone to record. Fortunately, Mrs. Heller made him put it away. Even though I was able to see the humor in the *Romeo and Juliet* mess, it didn't mean I wanted to give people an encore presentation to play back over and over again. One GroupIt hit was more than enough for me.

"Wes," Mrs. Heller said, "take it whenever you're ready. And you two feel free to move around, make up your own blocking, do what feels right."

What felt right was running back to my seat. But it was too late, Wes started reciting his lines. I was stuck. "Come, come, you wasp; i' faith . . ."

Wait. "I' faith." Seriously? If I wrote that in an English paper, Mrs. Heller would flunk me in a heartbeat. And they wondered why I had problems with Shakespeare-speak? It made no sense.

"You are too angry," he said.

What? He was calling me out on being angry now? I was going to kill him. Oh. Ha! Stupid me. It was his line. I needed to focus. It was my turn to read. Wes wasn't starting up with me here in front of the class. It was just part of the scene.

"If I be waspish, best beware my sting," I read. *Finally, a Shakespeare line I could understand.*

"My remedy is then, to pluck it out," he replied.

"Ay, if the fool could find it where it lies." Maybe this acting thing wasn't so hard after all. I just had to let my annoyance with Wes shine through. Maybe I wouldn't have hated Shakespeare so much if they had given me his snarky stuff first. Clearly, romance was not my strong suit.

I could feel Wes's eyes on me. "Who knows not where a wasp does wear his sting? In his tail." How was he not staring down at the paper the whole time? *Fine. Two could play at that game.* My next lines were short, I could look him right in the eyes as I said them, too.

"In his tongue."

"Whose tongue?" he answered.

Was I really talking about Wes's tongue? *Crap. I just looked at his lips. Back to his eyes, back to his eyes.*

"Yours, if you talk of tails: and so farewell," I said, and even threw in a little wave.

"What, with my tongue in your tail?" he said.

Whoa! Tongue in my tail? What were we reading? *Was my face red?* I hoped I wasn't red. Mrs. Heller's class should be renamed The Joys of Embarrassing Emily.

"Nay, come again, good Kate; I am a gentleman," Wes continued. Why was he so calm? *Because he doesn't like you, Emily. It's just lines to him.*

"That I'll try," I recited. The stage direction said "she strikes him," but I couldn't really hit him. Yeah, I was mad at him, but he was still Wes. Instead, I pretended. I pulled my hand back as if I were going in for a hard slap, but then I just softly cupped his cheek.

I finally understood that Romeo line where he was dreaming

of being Juliet's hand so he could touch her face. Being that close to Wes was nice, really nice. His eyes caught mine, and I was sure I felt something spark between us.

Then he placed his hand over mine, and I felt like one of those cartoon characters whose hearts beat a foot out of their chests.

"I swear I'll cuff you, if you strike again," he said, and moved my hand away.

Right. He was just acting. There was no spark. He was with Amanda. So much for being over him.

This time I kept my eyes solely on the paper. My emotions were too jumbled to look at Wes again. "So may you lose your arms: If you strike me, you are no gentleman; and if no gentleman, why then no arms."

"Great job," Mrs. Heller said. "Let's stop there. Let's give our actors a round of applause."

This time I didn't give a big bow or make a production, I just rushed back to my seat so I didn't have to stand next to Wes a second longer.

I scanned the part of the scene that we didn't get to. Petruchio actually picks Kate up and tries to carry her off. I wondered if Wes would have tried that. My body would have been pressed up against his. I'd get to feel him close to me. My arms wrapped around him. *Stop it, Emily. You don't like Wes. It's over with.* Maybe if I told myself that enough, it would be true.

I barely heard any of the other performances, my mind kept drifting back where it shouldn't have been. I tried to concentrate on Cody giving his Hamlet soliloquy, but my heart wasn't in it. I was relieved when the bell finally rang. It meant I got to go home and put this whole day behind me.

I shoved my things into my bag and raced for the door, but I wasn't fast enough. "Emily, wait up."

It was Wes. Why wouldn't he leave me alone? Did he want to torture me, rub it in my face that he liked Amanda?

"What?" I asked him.

"Can we talk? About earlier."

I kicked an imaginary scuff mark on the floor. I wasn't sure what he meant. Did he notice how visibly shaken I was when I found out he was going to the dance with Amanda? I decided to just play it breezy. "Everything's good."

"And us?" he asked.

"What about us?" The last I checked, there wasn't an us. There was an Amanda and him.

"Are we okay?"

"Why wouldn't we be?" I asked, and tried to smile. It felt fake, but it was all I could muster. I probably looked like the Joker from *Batman*.

"'Kay, just checking. Wouldn't want to lose my friend."

The freaking f-word. *Yeah, Wes, I get it. You're not into me. I'm just your friend. You don't need to remind me.*

"We're fine," I lied. I needed to get away from this conversation. I scanned the room. Standing right outside the door was Cody. I had to make a split-second decision. It was a no-brainer. I knew what I had to do. "Wes, I'm sorry, I have to run." Then I called out to Cody and told him to wait up.

"Glad you're still here," I told him, making sure to speak extraloud so Wes could hear the whole thing. I wanted to make sure my *friend* 100 percent understood that I didn't care whether he had feelings for me. I was now crushing on the most popular guy at school, at least that's what I needed Wes to believe.

"Your Hamlet was really good," I told Cody, making sure to put my hand on his arm as we spoke. "You could totally be an actor. Seriously. You have the look for it, too." *Were these words really coming out of my mouth? Puke.* I certainly hoped Wes was paying attention, because the groupie flattery I was spewing was going to make me sick.

"Yeah," Cody said, and flexed his bicep. "I've thought about modeling."

"You should do it." My hand was still on his arm. It was starting to get weird, but I couldn't take it away. Wes was still inside the classroom. I wasn't sure if he saw it.

"Don't know if I have time with football and everything."

"That makes sense."

Wes finally exited the room and walked by us.

"You're such an amazing player, Cody," I gushed. "You wouldn't want to do anything to jeopardize that. I love watching you on the field."

"Can't blame you," he said.

That would have been cute if he had been saying it to be funny. But I was pretty sure he meant it. Cody thought there was nothing better in life than Cody. By this point, I was confident Wes was out of earshot, which meant I didn't need to keep up the act anymore. Operation Pretend Flirt could take a rest. I dropped my hand and the supersickly sweet voice I was using. "All right. Bye, Cody." I turned and walked away.

"Wait, that's it?" he called after me.

"For now." It was a safe bet I'd turn the charm back on the next time Wes was around us. Cody looked half-confused, half-intrigued. Then it dawned on me. Cody Burns wasn't used to being dismissed by anyone. Except for with Amanda, he was the one who walked away first. But that was part of why I'd never really like someone like him. I didn't want games. I didn't want someone who thought everyone should cater to him. I wanted the nice guy. The cute, kind one who visited people in the hospital when they were sick and gave you a ride home when you were stuck at rehearsals late at night and didn't make you feel like a fool even when you acted like one. But that guy was no longer a possibility. My brain knew that. Now I just needed my heart to get the message.

23

The rest of the week proved to be a test of my patience and temper—basically it was a week of misery.

On the upside, I had been fairly successful at avoiding Wes. Sure, it meant sometimes turning around and walking in the opposite direction, hiding out until I was certain he was gone, and ducking into bathrooms, but it worked. I really only saw him in English.

We didn't speak in class, though. I always got there early enough to grab the seat in front of Cody, and I devoted all my attention to him. He may have thought I was crazy. Or maybe just two different people. In English class, I was all about him. I was flirty and chatty, and I oozed on the compliments. And when I saw him in geometry, chemistry, and Spanish (we had nearly every class together), we didn't really speak. I mean, I wasn't avoiding him the way I was avoiding Wes. I just wasn't putting in any extra effort. I said "hi" if I passed him, but that was about it. Although that was not entirely my fault. It wasn't like Cody went out of his way to talk to me, either. He always had a plethora of girls around him to stroke his ego, so it wasn't like he needed attention from me. I didn't really care, not as long as he kept flirting back in English class.

Amanda was my biggest problem. We had only history together. Thank goodness. I don't think I could have handled more than that. But for some reason, even though I should have seen her only in fifth period, it was as if she was everywhere I went. And when she wasn't there in body, her presence still loomed like a dark shadow I was fairly certain wanted to suck up my soul.

She'd try to rile me up, too. It was her favorite sport. Kayla and Jill told me to pretend Amanda didn't exist, to totally ignore her, that reacting would give her exactly what she wanted. I tried to take their advice and make the best of the situation. I didn't want her to win. So when I saw Amanda in the hall and she gave me that phony smile of hers, where her eyes shot darts at me, I just returned it. Each time. Even when she gushed over Wes right to my face, I kept my mouth shut. Even when she tried to kill my self-confidence, I still held back.

But Friday, when I got to English class, even though I was early, she was there—waiting outside the door. Her being there wasn't a surprise. It was becoming a daily occurrence, but I had always managed to get there before her. Now she had beaten me.

She flipped her hair over her shoulder. "Waiting for Wes," she informed me. But it seemed as if she was waiting for me. To rub my face in the fact that he wanted her. She was like a dog with a bone. She wouldn't let it drop.

"Good for you," I said, trying to act as nonchalant as I could muster. I was going to just walk past her, but then I noticed her focus shifted elsewhere. I turned to look. Cody was coming down the hall. And Amanda's gaze lingered on him just a little too long before she turned her attention back to me. She didn't think I caught it, but I did. Was there a chance she still liked him?

A gazillion thoughts flooded through me. If she liked him, this could be a win-win. Maybe she'd get rid of Wes, and he'd realize he wanted me. Not that I wanted to be second choice . . . but . . .

After all of Amanda's sly remarks to me about Wes, it was only fair that I got to turn the tables. "It must be weird for you to see Cody around," I said.

"Why would it be?"

"Well, I heard you took the breakup really hard." That was a lie. I was fishing. Rumor had it she broke it off, but I saw the look she just had on her face. It was the same one I got around Wes, and it told me there was way more to this story.

Her nostrils flared. "I dumped him."

I had struck a nerve. This was kind of fun. "Then you wouldn't care if he dated someone else?"

"Why would I?" she asked.

"Good to know."

Just then Cody got to the door. He gave a nod of acknowledgment to us both. He looked a little uncomfortable. I don't know if it was because his ex and the girl who was constantly hitting on him were talking, but the normally cool, collected façade he wore seemed slightly cracked.

As he passed us, I said, "See you in class, Cody," and I put my hand on his back.

"Oh my God," Amanda snorted when Cody was out of

138

earshot. "You do not think *you* have a chance with him, do you? I mean, look at him. And look at *you*."

"Oh, you'd be surprised. There's a lot you don't know, Amanda." As the bell rang, I called out to Cody. He turned, and I gave him a little wave and a wink. Wes's little habit (not that he'd done it to me in ages) was proving very effective. This time, there was no discomfort on Cody's face. He just gave me a huge grin and waved back.

I could tell Amanda was fuming, but she didn't say a word. I finally felt like I had beaten her at her own game, but my victory was short-lived. My Cody distraction made me lose track of time, and I was still standing at the door when Wes walked in. Amanda totally milked it. She gave him a kiss on the cheek, and even though I raced into the classroom, I could still hear them. Her laugh. Their talk about the dance. Her promise to meet him right after class.

English seemed to drag on. I was more than ready to go home once the bell rang. I had gotten avoiding Wes in class down to a science. (This had the surprising upside of increasing my English grade. I was getting tons of points for class participation.) I had two new standard exit strategies. If Wes was taking his time to pack up, I raced out of the room. If he got up quickly, I held back until I thought he was long gone. And Jill and Kayla tried not to leave me alone. They came to find me as soon as they could for backup support.

Today, Wes was the first one out of class, so I gave it four minutes and then exited. Only, he was still there. His back was up against the wall right next to the door, and Amanda was pressed into him. She was giggling and saying something, but I couldn't make it out. My head was foggy watching them.

"Emily," she said, once she caught sight of me. "Will we see you at the dance tonight? This guy here"—she crawled her fingers up his chest—"and I can't wait for tonight."

Wes looked almost as uncomfortable as I felt.

"You'll see all of us," Jill said, walking up, Kayla not too far behind.

Amanda waved her arm in a swishing motion. "Right, the group date. I guess when you can't get the real thing . . ."

"Or maybe," Kayla said, "it's the better way, and you just don't know what it's like to have friends who actually enjoy being around you."

We didn't wait for a response. Kayla just linked one of her elbows with mine, and Jill did the same. Then we turned and walked away.

Once we were finally outside, I felt as if I could breathe a little easier.

"Don't let her get you down," Kayla told me as we stood by the bike rack. "We'll have a great time at the dance."

I shook my head. "There's no way I'm going to that."

"You have to," Jill said.

"Why? So I can watch Wes and Amanda hold each other close, gaze into each other's eyes, and probably kiss? Or so I can be a fifth wheel and bug Kayla and Jace or ruin your first date with Seth? I wouldn't do that to you."

They spoke over each other. "You wouldn't be a fifth wheel," Kayla said right as Jill was telling me, "You wouldn't be ruining anything."

But they were just being nice. I knew I would destroy their nights. And not because you can't be single and go to a dance, but because I was going to be in a foul mood. How was I supposed to have fun with Amanda and Wes's relationship so in my face? I was going to be horrible company, and we all knew it. My friends, however, wouldn't listen to reason.

No matter how many rational arguments I made for why it was an incredibly bad idea for me to go to the dance, they wouldn't hear it.

"If you don't go, I'm not going," Jill said.

"You have to go. What about Seth?"

"I'll have to cancel."

I looked to Kayla. "Will you talk some sense into her? She's not doing that because of me."

Kayla shrugged. "You don't go, none of us go. We're not letting you sit home and sulk by yourself."

"Stop it," I said. "This isn't going to make me feel better. I want you guys to go to the dance. You've both been looking forward to it. You'll have fun there. I won't. Seriously, I will be okay by myself for a night. I'll get in comfy pajamas, watch Netflix, eat whatever I want. It will be great."

"Does sound great." Jill leaned against the bike rack. "So we'll join you then."

I clenched my hands into fists. They were not ruining their night because of me. Especially not Jill. I knew how excited she was about her date. I had been watching her and Seth in study hall. I had moved a couple of rows behind them so Jill could have some alone time with him, and seeing them together made my heart all melty. They were totally adorable. They'd each sneak peeks at the other one when they thought no one was looking. And Seth kept lifting his arm as if he was going to go in and take her hand, but then he kept pulling back. He was nervous. This date was exactly what they needed. I was not going to be the one to take that from them.

"Ever think I just need some time alone?" I asked them.

Kayla shook her head. "No, not really. You're stuck with us, but where we hang out is up to you."

I shoved my hands into my pockets. "Fine. I'll go to the dance. But I'm not ruining either of your dates. I'll have one of my parents drive me. I'll meet you there. I'm not tagging along in the car with either of you. Deal?"

"Deal," they both said.

They hadn't given me any choice. I had to tell them what they wanted to hear. But it was all going to work out. They'd forgive me when I didn't show up. Besides, it didn't really count as lying if my fingers were crossed the whole time, right?

24

"Isn't the school dance tonight?" my mom asked as I fished through the refrigerator in my I-hate-life Friday night bests, which consisted of baggy red sweatpants and a faded Cleveland Browns T-shirt.

"What?" How did she know?

"You left one of those flyers lying around," she said, reading my mind.

"I'm not going."

"Why not?"

"Sick," I answered.

She eyed my stash of food. Leftover lasagna, two chocolate puddings, and a Coke. "Pretty healthy appetite for someone who isn't feeling well."

"Feed a fever, starve a cold," I told her. I didn't want this conversation. I just wanted to take food—a lot of it—and hide in my room for the rest of the night—the rest of my life if it was possible—and never think of Wes Rosenthal again.

"Emily, what's going on?" she asked. "You've been upset all week. Is this about that production you did? I've been trying not to ask you about it, but something's obviously bothering you."

A pudding dropped out of my hand. She couldn't know about the *Romeo and Juliet* scene, could she? "What production?"

"The one that's all over your GroupIt page."

Shoot. Why had I accepted my mother's follow request? I winced as I bent over to pick up my snack. "That, ummm, that was nothing."

"It didn't look like nothing. It looked like you didn't learn your lines. Emily, are you in trouble at school? Talk to me."

"I don't want to talk," I said, my voice getting louder, but she just kept looking at me. "Fine. You want to know? I'll tell you. I'll tell you everything. I wasn't even supposed to be on that stage. I didn't want to do it. But I did. And I made a fool of myself. But then Wes . . . Wes . . ." I was yelling now. "I thought he liked me . . . but he didn't . . . he chose . . ." I couldn't finish. Everything from the past few weeks, the play, Amanda's insults, Wes going to the dance with Amanda all hit me at once, and I broke down into sobs.

"Okay, okay," my mom said, her voice low. She put her arm around me and squeezed. "It will be all right."

"No, it won't."

She gave me a hug and let me cry into her shoulder. "Trust me," she said after a few minutes. "You'll get through this. If this guy can't see how truly amazing you are, you don't need him. Emily, you are special. You have so much heart. You're smart and you're strong and you have your dad's knack for finding the positive in everything. I've always admired that about you."

I wanted her to be right, but she wasn't. "There's no positive in this."

"You'll find it."

"I'm not so sure about that." She kissed the top of my head, and I got an idea that would definitely cheer me up. "If you got me a car . . ."

She reached into the drawer. "Nice try," she said, and handed me a spoon. "But I'll be here for you, always, and for tonight I won't even give you a hard time about eating in your bedroom."

While I would have preferred the car, I was going to take what I could get. I went to my room, dumped my food stash on the desk next to my bed, and pulled out my laptop. It was time for some binge watching and eating. The dance didn't start until eight, so I had a good hour and a half until my friends started blowing up my phone, asking me where I was. But they'd understand why I didn't show. I wanted them to have fun with their dates and not worry about me.

I was only half an hour into my first show when my bedroom door burst open. "Mom!"

Only, it wasn't my mom. It was Jill and Kayla. "Huh?!! What are you doing here and dressed like that? I mean, you guys look beautiful, but you shouldn't be *here*." They really did look great. Jill was wearing an emerald-green slip dress that made her eyes pop, and her hair was curled and swept into an intentionally messy side bun. She truly looked stunning. Kayla too. Her hair was in a boho halo braid that made her look like a Renaissance princess, and she was wearing an aqua dress that rested just above her knees and had these incredible lace bell sleeves. It looked as if it was made for her, and then I realized it probably was. "Did you design that?"

"Yep," she said. "Sewed it myself, too."

"Wow," I said. "You're both breathtaking. Seriously."

"You can fan-girl all you want later, Cinderella, but right now Jill and I have our fairy godmother work cut out for us."

"What?" I said again. "No. You guys need to go. The dance is at eight. You have more important things to do."

"No, we don't," Jill said.

Kayla dropped her bag on my floor. "We're all ready for the dance. That leaves an hour to work on you."

"Guys, I really don't want to go."

"You promised us you'd be there," Jill said.

"I only said that because you wouldn't take no for an answer."

Kayla took a seat in my desk chair. "Look, we knew you were going to flake on us. But there was no way we were going to let you sit here and sulk and feel sorry for yourself while we were at the dance. So we came here to make sure you got your butt over there."

"And worst-case scenario," Jill added, sitting on the edge of my bed, "we'll just drag you there. You're not getting out of this."

"Guys, I appreciate everything you're trying to do. I really do. But I just want to be alone. I promise you, it's better this way. I'm going to be crappy company."

"So what else is new?" Kayla said.

"Very funny," I shot back. "Please, just forget about me for one night."

Jill put her no-nonsense voice to use. "You know that's not going to happen. We can either spend an hour convincing you to go with us—which you eventually will. Or we can save time, you can just agree to it now, and you can start to get ready."

"Jill!"

"We're serious, Em. I will stand Seth up over this. You want to be responsible for that?"

I really didn't. "Even if I wanted to go," I said. "I can't. I'm a mess. I don't have anything to wear to a semiformal." Instead of a fun, cool, low-maintenance night out, Amanda's brainstorm was that we all needed to wear uncomfortable clothing and shoes and pretend we were way fancier than we really were. We already had homecoming and prom (well, for the upper-classmen, anyway). How many fancy dances did we need? "I know I said I was going to wear that powder-blue lacy thing from my cousin's bat mitzvah, but the truth is, that hasn't fit in about a year. Ben & Jerry saw to that."

"Well, lucky for you," Kayla said, "one of your very best friends in the whole wide world is an awesome dress designer and has you covered." I hated to admit it, but I was starting to get a little excited as Kayla pulled out a dress from her bag. Her stuff was always amazing.

"Here you go," she said. "A Kayla Nunez original."

"Wow!" It was a sleeveless rose-colored gown with a draped asymmetrical peplum at the waist. And while it was long, the bottom was a wrap skirt with a slit at the front. I couldn't believe I was going to get to wear this dress.

"Kayla, that's incredible," Jill said.

"Thank you very much. What are you waiting for?" she asked me. "Put it on."

I held the dress for a minute, feeling the delicate cloth between my fingers, then decided what the hell. I saw Wes and

Amanda every day at school—who cared if they were at the dance? I couldn't let them ruin my night.

I tried it on, but they wouldn't let me look at myself just yet. They wanted me to see only the final version, probably so I wouldn't be all critical and question their every move. Jill was on hair. She twisted it into a bun at the nape of my neck and pulled out a few tendrils to frame my face while Kayla tried to give me some kind of smoky-eye look. The last time I tried that, I looked like a raccoon, but Kayla was better at that kind of thing than I was, so I tried to have a little faith.

Then they put a hammered silver necklace around my neck. It was thick and textured, and as Kayla put it, "a statement piece to go with the dress—adds to the open neckline." Then they completed the look with delicate ruby earrings. They were fakes, but you couldn't really tell, at least I couldn't.

"Okay," Kayla said. "All set."

When they finally pulled out a mirror and let me look at myself, I was taken aback. I looked good. I mean, I still looked like me, but a fancier, much more put-together version. And the dress, it left me at a loss for words. It gave me just the right amount of cleavage and made my waist look great.

"You look perfect," Jill said.

I kind of did, if I did say so myself. I spun around to get a better look.

"Ewww," Kayla said.

"What?"

"Your feet. You don't wear a gown and socks. I know you must own at least one nice pair of shoes."

I rummaged through my closet and found a cute pair of

ballet slippers (I wasn't big on heels) and held them up for Kayla's approval.

She gave it.

"Then it looks like it's time to go," Jill said.

"Wait." I had something I had to say first. "This week has been awful, but you guys were there for me the whole time. You're . . ." My eyes started to well up.

"Don't cry," Kayla ordered, but I saw her eyes get dewy as well. "It took me forever to get your makeup just right."

"It's just, you two are the best. Thank you."

"Okay, you guys are going to make me cry, too," Jill said, and started wiping at the corners of her eyes.

I tried to compose myself. "No tears. We look too good," I said with a laugh. "But just know I love you both. I don't know what I'd do without you. Seriously."

"Me too," Jill said, and grabbed us both in a hug.

"Me three," Kayla said, "but we need to get out of here now, before I have to redo all our makeup. So enough with this mushy stuff. Let's go dance!"

She ushered us out of my room and downstairs. My mom let out a whistle when she saw us. "Gorgeous, ladies. So I guess you're feeling better, Em?" she asked.

I nodded.

"I knew you would." She came over and gave me a kiss on my cheek, careful not to mess up Kayla's kick-ass contouring work. "Have fun tonight."

And the thing was, I was pretty sure I would.

Because while I might not have had any luck when it came to guys, when it came to friends, I definitely took home the top prize.

25

"Ready to make your entrance, Cinderella?" Kayla asked when we got to the dance.

It was already after eight, so the dance was well under way. There was a pretty good chance that everyone who was going to be there was already inside. Including Amanda and Wes. I took a deep breath. I could do this.

"Yeah, I think I am."

Jill opened the door and gestured for me to enter. "After you."

I stepped inside. The room actually looked kind of nice. It was just the cafeteria, but it was transformed. The tables were pushed to the walls. White tablecloths with black napkins and cups covered them, and they were filled with snacks. And it looked as if Amanda (well, technically me, since I had to pick them up for her) had bought out a balloon factory. There were white and black balloons everywhere. In an arc over the dee-jay, flying above the tables, and tons of loose ones floating around the ground. I picked one up, and Kayla bopped it out of my hands. "It's covering your dress. Cleavage like yours should be seen."

"Nice," I said. I grabbed another balloon and threw it at her. She hit it back, and Jill jumped in to continue the volley. If I could have stayed tucked away by the entrance with them all night just hitting balloons, I'd definitely be able to survive the evening, but I knew that wasn't possible.

Seth immediately spotted Jill and came right over. "There you are," he said, his face breaking into a giant grin. He really liked her. You could almost feel how much. "You look really pretty."

"Thanks," she said, her voice low. She was positively glowing. "You look good, too."

He couldn't stop smiling at her. I swear they were the most adorable couple ever. He must have realized we were all watching them, because he nodded at us in greeting. "Hi."

"Hey," I said back.

It got quiet. The uncomfortable kind. And I was the reason. Seth obviously wanted to ask Jill to dance, but he wasn't going to. Not with me there. Jill undoubtedly filled him in on what was going on, and he was a nice guy. He wasn't going to try to get her to pawn me off on someone else, so he could have her to himself. Not that she would. She was too good a friend. So it was up to me.

"I thought you promised to teach Seth how to dance?" I asked.

"I will later," she said.

"That's not good enough. You better get out there now. This is a perfect dance song."

Jill looked torn over whether to stay or go.

"Come with us?" Seth asked.

"Yes," Kayla answered for us both, and she grabbed my arm

151

and led our little group to the center of the dance floor. A fast song was playing, and they all started dancing, while I scanned the room for you know who. But there was no sign of Amanda or Wes. I wasn't sure if that was good or bad. I didn't want to see them, but I had a superactive imagination, and the thought of them kissing in some empty classroom bothered me even more than the idea of seeing them dancing together.

"You know you have to actually move your body to dance?" Jace informed me as he joined our group and gave Kayla a quick kiss hello. Then they each grabbed one of my arms and started waving them up and down as if I were a marionette.

"I get it," I said, and actually began to dance. Like, really dance. Like, forget-my-problems-and-lose-them-to-the-beat dance. The deejay played four fast songs before he broke it up with a slow one. I was actually a little out of breath by that point.

"I'm going to go grab a drink," I told everyone. "I'll be right back." I didn't give them time to stop me, I just took off. They shouldn't have to quit dancing and sit out all the slow songs because I didn't have a date. I could fend for myself. I was self-sufficient. I had other friends at this school. I didn't need a babysitter. At least that's what I was trying to tell myself.

As I walked over to the refreshment stand, I caught a few people staring at me. I smoothed out my dress. Were they looking because they thought I looked good? Or because I was the girl who made a fool of herself on Shakespeare in the Heights Night? I'd probably never find out (not that I really wanted to know), so I decided to just take it as a compliment even if it wasn't.

The song was taking forever to end. I poured myself a

cup of punch as slowly as I possibly could and started to nurse it. Maybe by the time I was finished, another fast song would start up.

Only, no such luck. It was another romantic ballad. I should have known. Amanda warned me the night was geared toward couples. And she would know. She was in charge; she probably made the set list herself.

As I poured myself another drink, someone behind me cleared his throat.

I turned around to see Wes's brother, Neal, staring at me.

He bowed and put out one hand, "Excuse-eth moi, my lady. But may-eth I have this dance?"

Was this really happening?

I knew he wasn't trying to be rude with the Shakespeare-speak. He was trying to be cute, but it just came off as awkward. I couldn't say yes to Neal. I'd look like a fool out on the dance floor with him. I was four years older, considerably taller, and already had that stupid GroupIt incident hanging over my head. Yet I didn't really want to turn him down, either. Okay, I did, but I didn't want to hurt his feelings. Especially not after I overheard that conversation. And Wes had told me Neal was having a hard time fitting in, and a dance like this had to be superhard for him. But he was here anyway and taking a risk by asking me to dance.

Wait? He didn't really think I liked him, did he?

I studied his face. I couldn't tell, but at least he didn't bring up my tagging myself in his picture.

I could just say no. I was asking for more mocking by dancing with him to a slow song. But he was Wes's brother. And it was just one dance.

I didn't know what to do. Say no? Wait for a fast song? Pretend Kayla and Jill were waiting for me? It turned out I didn't have to do any of that, my delayed response was answer enough.

Neal smiled sadly. "It's okay," he said. "I get it."

He turned away.

"Neal, wait," I called after him. I put out my hand. "I'd be happy to dance with you."

"Really?" he asked.

I nodded, and his face lit up.

"Thanks," he said, and took my hand.

I figured, why not? I knew how bad rejection hurt. And he wasn't asking me to be his girlfriend or to kiss him or to run away to Boston. It was just a dance. Besides, after all I'd been through the past few weeks, there really wasn't anything that could embarrass me anymore. Let people make fun of me if they wanted to. I didn't care. Besides, this wasn't anything to be ashamed of. I was dancing with my friend's (or whatever he was) brother. My night might have been a bust, but maybe I could help make someone else's a little better.

I put my hands on his shoulders, and he wrapped his arms around my waist, but I made sure there was a good six or so inches between us. With our height difference and the dress pushing my chest up, Neal was virtually eye level with my cleavage. I probably should have thought about that before I said yes.

Even though he kept his eyes on mine, it was still a pretty uncomfortable two minutes for me, but I made sure to keep a smile on the whole time. When the song finally ended, he gave me a sheepish grin. "Thanks again," he said. "You're the only girl who said yes all night." I got the feeling his rejections had been in the double digits.

I squeezed his arm. "It will get easier. Right now you're the youngest, but there'll be a new class next year. And I bet you could still go to the middle school dances if you wanted. Then you'd be around people your age, but you'd be the mysterious high school guy who got to get out of two years of school."

He laughed. "Maybe I'll give that a try. Thanks again."

As we were standing there, Wes came up and slapped his hand on his brother's shoulder. "Hey," he said, and Neal nodded at him.

"Mom texted me," Wes told him. "She's outside. She said you weren't answering. Now I can see why."

"Oh, I better go. See you later, Wes. Thanks again, Emily." He waved and left me and Wes standing there.

"So you and my brother, huh? First the picture, now the dance?"

"It's not like that. You know the whole GroupIt thing was an accident. I didn't mean to—"

"I know. I'm kidding," he said. "I appreciate what you did. I heard what you said to him. It meant a lot. To him, and to me."

Stop it, Wes. You can't say things like that. It doesn't help me get over you.

"It wasn't a big deal."

"Yeah, it was. I was supposed to give him a ride home tonight, but he called our mom to pick him up early because he was having a horrible time. You made his night."

I didn't know what to say, or where to look, or what to think. "I'm glad I could help."

Wes's eyes roamed over my dress, and I felt all my muscles tighten at once. Was he checking me out?

"You look good. Really good. You always do, though."

He *had* been checking me out. *Okay, Wes, you really need to cut it out.*

"Have you been having fun?" he asked.

"It's been okay," I said, trying to keep my tone friendly, like I wasn't fazed at all, even though he was totally messing with my head. "Your brother was the first person to ask me to dance all night if that tells you anything."

His eyes looked thoughtful. "I'm sure a lot of guys were dying to ask."

This REALLY needed to end. What guys, Wes? You? You who didn't want me? You who picked another girl?!! Do you like seeing me squirm? Is that what this is? Well, forget it. You made your decision, you don't get to keep me pining for you while you go off living happily ever after with my least favorite person on the planet. But . . . what if he realized he made a mistake? What if he knew Amanda was the wrong choice?

"Thanks," I said. Why was he so confusing?

"Found you," Amanda said, sidling right up to Wes. It was as if just thinking her name summoned the devil. Of course she had to show up now. "Emily," she said, acknowledging me, but just barely.

"Hi, Amanda."

I looked for an out, for anyone I recognized, but none appeared.

Wes looked uncomfortable. But that's expected when your girlfriend catches you hitting on someone else. I really was an idiot. For a moment I seriously thought he might have wanted me over her. I was such a fool.

The music changed to yet another slow song, and Amanda pulled Wes to the dance floor. "I love this one. Come dance." I tried to ignore my emotions as I watched her put her arms around his neck and slide up close to him.

I felt so alone. Then it got worse. Amanda turned and gave me the most pitying look I had ever seen. My blood started to boil.

I grabbed my phone from my purse and sent out a quick text.

Not even sixty seconds later, Cody was standing in front of me, one eyebrow raised. "So you really want to dance with me, huh?" he asked, reciting part of my text back to me. The rest of it said: **Don't keep me waiting.**

"I really do," I said, and took his hand and led him to the dance floor, right next to Wes and Amanda.

Cody pulled me close to him, and we swayed softly to the music. His hands started to wander a little too low, but I nudged them back to my waist. He leaned down and whispered in my ear, "You look hot tonight."

"So do you," I answered.

I knew Amanda must have been seething.

When the song ended, I told Cody I had to get going, that my ride was leaving soon.

"I can drive you," he offered, his hands resting on my hips. "We can hang out."

I glanced over. Wes and Amanda were definitely watching us. Amanda looked as if she were going to spit fire in my direction. And Wes looked confused. *Good, now they know how it feels.* A rush went through me, and before I could stop myself, I said something I knew I would regret.

"Not tonight, but how about we get together next week? Maybe dinner Wednesday?" I asked.

"Dinner?" He looked slightly disappointed. I think he had been hoping for more of a Netflix and Chill night, but I was more of a let's-eat-pizza-and-get-to-know-each-other-in-a-public-place kind of girl.

I nodded.

"Yeah, okay," he said.

"Great, it's a date," I said, and kissed him on the cheek.

And just like that I had plans with the guy of my dream's girlfriend's ex. I turned back around to face Wes and Amanda and smiled. From now on, they weren't going to be the only two flaunting their new relationship. Cody and I were going to be the new it couple. Emdy or Comily. Whatever, it didn't matter, not as long as people knew it existed.

26

"Tell me again what you were thinking?" Jill asked as she drove me to my date with Cody.

We had been through this a thousand times since the dance. "I don't know. It just seemed like a good idea at the time."

Not long after I proposed the idea of a date with Cody, I knew it was a bad one. I just wanted to make Amanda jealous. That look she gave me set me off. And even though she and Cody were long over, I knew she wouldn't want to see her ex with someone else. Especially if that someone was me. She had been torturing me about her relationship with Wes for weeks. Payback seemed like the way to go. Especially with Wes right there with his arms wrapped around her. For a moment, I thought that if he knew I had a date with someone else, he'd get jealous, too. But I hadn't thought about what my decision meant. Now I had to spend a whole night out with Cody. Our conversations in school lasted five minutes max. Trying to stretch that over the course of an entire evening was going to be impossible—or at the very least tedious. But there was no backing out now. Amanda and Wes would find out, and that would have defeated the whole purpose of setting up the date in the first place. I could handle one night.

"Here we are," Jill said as we pulled up in front of Serio's, an Italian restaurant in town.

"Thanks for taking me tonight," I said. Cody didn't offer to pick me up, and I really didn't want my parents to drive me to my date. Not that that was really an option. It was Wednesday night, and they had some card tournament they took part in.

"No problem. Want me to wait in the car for a bit?" Jill asked.

I looked at the time. 7:14. I was meeting Cody at seven thirty. I was way early.

"Thanks, it's okay. I know your mom will start freaking out if you're not home soon. I'll be fine." The drive over was quicker than I thought. I had hoped to get to Serio's after Cody. I didn't want to look too eager, as if I had been waiting all day for this. I didn't even like him. There was a slight chance he was already inside, and we could get this date over with, but I doubted I was that lucky.

Too bad Kayla and Jace weren't here yet. They were going to show up around eight, and if I really needed to get away from Cody, we had a signal and they'd come rescue me.

There was no putting it off. I had to go inside. I thanked Jill again and got out of the car. I'd walked into Serio's a gazillion times, only this time it felt different, as if I were a death row prisoner who was about to get her final meal. Okay, I was exaggerating slightly. Dinner with Cody was probably not going to be *that* bad. But I could hardly expect it to be good.

I bypassed the host and walked to the back of the restaurant. It was fairly empty. There was no sign of Cody, so instead of grabbing a table, I just took a quick right and decided to hide in the ladies' room for a bit.

I looked in the mirror and tried to tame my frizz while I waited. It felt as if I'd been in there forever, but when I looked at my phone, it had been only three minutes. The restroom wasn't giant, but it was big enough to pace, which is what I did next. *Why hadn't I just canceled?* But this evening was probably good for me. A date was probably exactly what I needed to get over Wes, and maybe I wasn't giving Cody enough credit. Maybe he was supercharming and nice and not 100 percent narcissistic when you got him outside of school.

I heard the door next to me (the men's room) open and a voice that sounded a lot like Cody's say, "You go to University Heights, don't you?" University Heights was the high school in the town next door.

"Yeah, how did you know?" a girl's voice answered.

"You're on the cheerleading squad. I've seen you. You're hard to miss."

She giggled.

"But," he added, "you're cheering for the wrong side."

"Is that so?" she asked, her voice playful.

"Yep. But maybe I'll be able to convince you to switch sides."

Oh. My. God. My date was flirting with another girl right here in the restaurant. This was a great way to start the evening. I couldn't believe he was doing this. I took a deep breath. *Relax, Emily.* It was fine. I mean, we were hardly exclusive. I didn't even really like him. But still . . . he had to hit on someone here? He couldn't wait until the next football game between Shaker Heights and University Heights to pick her up? This was going to be embarrassing. She was probably going to sit at the table next to us, too. I hoped this evening wouldn't turn out worse than I had imagined.

I jumped when someone knocked on the bathroom door.

Shoot. Someone needed to use it, but I couldn't walk out now. What if Cody was still standing there? I didn't want him to know I had heard him. It would just make the whole night awkward. At least for me. He probably wouldn't care. "Just a minute," I said, lowering my voice, hoping to disguise it.

I flushed the toilet for good measure, ran the faucet a minute to buy myself some more time, and then I stepped out. Fortunately, Cody wasn't there. He had gone back into the dining area. Only, he wasn't alone. He was standing there with Wes and Amanda.

This could not be happening.

I ran my fingers through my hair to get out any last clumps and tugged down on my dress. It was a little too short, but it was the first one I had pulled out of my closet. Why hadn't I put in more effort to get ready? If I knew Wes was going to be here, I definitely would have.

Put on a smile, put on a smile, I reminded myself as I approached them. I had to up my game. It didn't matter that Cody had just hit on some random girl. I needed to pretend I was head over heels. I could do it. Fortunately for me, my fake-flirting skills were a lot better than my acting ones. "Hey, everyone." I went over and kissed Cody on the cheek for good measure. He pulled me in closer, wrapping his arm around me. It caught me off guard. If he hadn't been practically holding me up, I would have lost my balance. "Wes, Amanda," I said, "what are you doing here?"

"Having dinner," she answered.

"Right, that makes sense. Silly question," I started blithering. "What else would you be doing here? That's why Cody and I are here. Dinner. It's really good. Cleveland's best three years running. At least as far as I know. It's—"

"Are you all together?" the waitress interrupted.

"Yeah, why not," I said without really thinking it through. No one looked happy about the idea. Amanda's nostrils even flared, but she didn't say anything.

"Right this way," the waitress said, and took us to a table for four near the middle of the room.

"The more the merrier, right?" I said.

"Yeah," Wes answered, unconvincingly. This was a nightmare. As soon as Kayla got there, I would use the signal. But I couldn't. Then Amanda would know I wasn't really into Cody. Great, I was going to be stuck on this date all night.

Wes took the seat across from Amanda, and Cody sat next to her. That meant I would be facing Cody and to the left of Wes. I wished I were on a date with him. *No, you don't*, I reminded myself. *He chose Amanda.* It was even more reason to make the best of the situation and flirt up a storm with Cody.

"Don't you look handsome," I said, and winked at Cody. I hoped Wes saw it and realized how annoying winking was when you weren't on the receiving end.

"Always do," he answered, and winked back. That was not exactly the response I was looking for in return. It wasn't that I needed a compliment from him, I just thought it would have been nice. Well, nice for Amanda and Wes to overhear anyway.

"And that's a great color on you, Amanda." If I had to sit at a table with her all evening, at least I could try to get on her good side. Maybe it would make the night somewhat bearable. Besides, the deep blue really did look nice on her.

"It's one of my favorites," she said.

No thank-you from her, either. Nor did she try to push the conversation forward. No wonder she and Cody broke up, they probably both just sat there waiting for one to tell the other how amazing he or she looked.

"Well, you look really pretty," I told her as I sat down.

"You do, too," Wes said to me.

Amanda's eyes narrowed at him ever so slightly.

I couldn't look at Wes. I knew he was just trying to be polite, but I still turned to mush when he said things like that. "Thanks."

Then it got awkwardly silent. You'd think with four people sitting there, one of us would have had something to say, but you'd be wrong.

"So . . ." I tried to break the ice. "Do you guys know what you want?"

"Want to just share a pizza?" Wes asked.

No one seemed to object, so a cheese pizza it was.

The manager, Sal, came over and told us that our waitress would be back in a minute but that he'd get us started on drinks. Wes got a water, Amanda and Cody got Coke, and I got an orange pop.

When he walked away, it got quiet again.

It was a relief when the waitress took our order, but that deafening silence returned when she left.

"I love this place," I said, attempting one more time to get some kind of conversation going. "They really do have the best pizza in town."

"And the cutest waitresses, too, right, Cody?" Amanda asked.

"Not this again," he said.

What was going on? Was the girl Cody was flirting with before a waitress? Had Amanda seen it? Was she just trying to make me feel uncomfortable? If she was, it was working.

"I figured the one upside of breaking up was at least I wouldn't have to listen to this crap anymore," he muttered.

Whoa. This wasn't about me. Apparently, Cody must have had a habit of flirting with other people in front of his dates.

"Crap?" she said, her eyes turning into little slits.

I could not believe they were having this conversation in front of Wes and me.

"Yeah," he said. "You don't answer a single call or text for like a month, and now you want to do this here? Now?"

"So." I turned to Wes. "Have you been here before?" I asked, pretending our dates weren't causing a scene.

"My family comes here all the time," Wes said, acting as if it were just the two of us. "I agree about the pizza, but my mom is crazy about their pasta. And my dad and brother would kill for their triple-chocolate blackout cake."

"I've never had it."

"Well, then we're definitely ordering it tonight."

"What's that about chocolate cake?" Amanda interrupted, turning her focus back to us. Apparently, her Cody fight was on hold, and she was pretending as if it hadn't happened. Cody just sat there sulking.

I thought about suggesting we get another table. But we ordered together, and okay, I'll admit, I liked being there with

Wes. And it was nice not being the only problem causer for once.

"Was just saying how good it is," Wes said.

The waitress brought over our drinks, but Cody didn't even dare look at her. But when she left, it was as if something snapped to life in him, and all of a sudden I was his sun and moon.

"You know, Em, I don't think I told you how pretty you look. That dress makes your eyes sparkle." He was laying it on strong, but he actually sounded sincere. He even gave me this sexy little half smile, where he bowed his head and then looked up at me through his thick lashes with his big puppy dog eyes. "I'm really glad we're doing this tonight." Deep down, I had a feeling he was using me for Amanda's benefit, the way I was using him for Wes's. That being said, he was convincing. He kind of oozed charm when he wanted to. Combine that with how hot he was, no wonder he got so many girls. I wasn't truly falling for his act, but it had the potential to make the rest of the evening a lot more enjoyable. Who didn't like compliments?

"Me too," I said.

Then he reached over and took my hand with his left one and touched my knee with his right! Whoa, whoa, WHOA! Fake praise was one thing. Touching was a whole other category that we were not going to explore. There was no way I was letting that continue. I yanked my hand and knee away from him. Only, I was a little thrown off guard from the situation and wasn't paying attention when I jerked away, and I wound up knocking over my orange pop. It spilled right onto my dress. Just when I thought I was all embarrassed out, that nothing could get to me again, I was proved wrong.

Amanda jumped back from the table. "That better not have gotten on me. This outfit cost a fortune."

I rolled my eyes. It was nowhere near her. I was the mess. If anything, the collateral damage would have been Wes. He was the one next to me. "I'm sorry. Did I get it on you?"

"No, I'm good," he said, trying to hold up the tablecloth so more of the liquid wouldn't rain down on me.

The waitress brought over more napkins to soak up the spill. I started blotting my dress, and Wes tried to clean up the rest of the table.

"You have some right here," he said, and held the napkin on the fabric right above my knee. His thumb grazed my skin.

It was different from when Cody did it. I actually quivered from Wes's touch. A good kind of quiver. "Thanks, I got it."

"Yeah, of course," he said, quickly pulling away. "Sorry."

"Nothing to be sorry for." *Unless it was his liking Amanda over me.* "I'm going to go wash up. I'll be right back."

I didn't even want to think about what the conversation at the table would be like once I was gone. Amanda snarking about what a klutz I was, Cody laughing over my reaction to a little touch, and Wes—well, I had no idea what he'd say. Maybe he'd just have to listen to them fighting some more or bonding over making fun of me.

I locked the bathroom door (I was spending way too much time in there this evening) and pulled off the dress. I hoped I hadn't ruined it. It wasn't my favorite in the whole world, but I still liked it.

I cupped my hands and filled them with water, which I tried to pour over just the spots. I wasn't very successful. Water splattered everywhere. And because the dress was such a light shade of pink, you could see every drop. I was going to look a mess when I went back out there. At least I was making Amanda's night better. Every disaster for me was a win for her.

This night couldn't end soon enough. I hoped that by the time I went back out, the pizza would be there, then we could just eat and leave. I looked at the dress. It seemed like I got it all out. I'd go over it again when I got home. Before I put the dress back on, I decided I might as well use the toilet since I was already in there.

No sooner had I sat down and started my business, there was a knock on the door.

"Em, are you okay?"

It was Wes.

Could he hear me pee? Uck. Why was my life a constant disaster? "Fine, be right out," I called to him.

"Do you need anything?"

Yeah, you to leave me alone right now so I could go to the bathroom in peace.

"Nope, I'm good."

"Okay," he said. "Just wanted to check."

"Thanks." Oh my God. Did I let out a fart? No! Did he hear it? This kind of thing did not happen to girls on the CW or Freeform shows. Hell, *they* didn't even go to the bathroom let alone have the guy of their dreams calling to them while they sat on the toilet. Why couldn't I be a character on a TV show? My life would be so much easier. I would definitely take being a vampire or a superhero over being a pathetic klutz.

I finished as fast as I could, washed my hands, and threw on my dress. When I opened the door, I was relieved to see that Wes wasn't there.

I walked back into the main dining room and saw Kayla and Jace sitting near the back, about three tables behind my group. They must have arrived while I was in the bathroom. I gave them a little wave as I walked by.

"Emily," Kayla gasped. "Your dress."

The giant water marks were impossible to miss. "I know," I whispered, "and this was one of the better things that happened tonight. I'll tell you later."

When I got back to my table, the pizza was already there. I grabbed a slice and shoved it into my mouth. If I was chewing, I wasn't talking and risking making a bigger fool of myself. Besides, the quicker the food was gone, the quicker I got to go home.

"You sure know how to make yourself the center of attention," Cody said.

"Not intentionally," I told him. "I'd much rather stay out of the spotlight. Amanda can have it."

"I will Friday," she said. "When Wes and I do our scene."

She reached out and took his hand. Only, he didn't jerk away the way I did when Cody tried to take mine. I jammed another bite of pizza into my mouth. Amanda certainly seemed in a better mood. I guess my embarrassment lifted her spirits.

"It's going to be so great," she said. "We've been rehearsing, and let me tell you, our scene is going to sizzle." She turned toward me and Cody. "It's really hot."

"Yeah, I got that from the sizzle part," I answered, my mouth still full of food. While I didn't like talking about Amanda and Wes, it beat focusing on my klutziness. I was just grateful Amanda's need to brag outweighed her need to ridicule me.

"I even got Ryan to help me with that long monologue, my blocking, my characterization. He totally reworked everything. It's so much better than the way I was doing it before."

"Wait, what?" I asked. "You changed Jill's scene? She worked really hard on that."

"It's not a big deal. *Ryan* won best director. I figured the best for the best."

"He only won," I said, trying to hold back my anger, "because no one got to see Jill's actual scene. You weren't there, remember?" I could not believe she was doing this to my best friend. This was supposed to be Jill's second chance, too.

"My stuff is all the same," Wes added.

Amanda glared at him and then turned back to me. "If I want help with my acting so I can give an unrivaled performance, that's my business. *I'm* the one up there. Not Jill."

I was at a loss for words, but Amanda wasn't. She kept going like she hadn't just dropped a major bomb on me.

She turned to Cody. "The whole eleventh grade is getting out of last period so they can come watch. You'll love that."

"Yeah, anything that gets me out of class," he said.

She rolled her eyes.

I was so annoyed. I kept silent as they all made small talk about the scene and Amanda's goals of being a famous actress until we finally finished the pizza.

"Anything else?" the waitress asked us.

"Just the check," I said.

"What about the triple-chocolate blackout cake?" Wes asked.

"Not tonight," I answered. Cake sounded good, but after

everything—the fighting, the spilling, the directing news—leaving sounded better. I think he understood that.

When the check arrived, Wes picked it up. "Cody, why don't you and I just split it?"

"Why?" Cody answered. "I didn't eat half the food."

"Because it's the nice thing to do," Amanda informed him.

I was shocked she was saying that. But then again, she had already shown us that her resentment for Cody outweighed her disgust for me.

"This isn't the fifties. If anything," Cody said, "Emily should be paying for me. She's the one who suggested dinner. I just wanted to hang out."

Amanda rolled her eyes again. "After the night she had, you'd think you could at least buy her some pizza."

"I'll take care of it," Wes said. "It's not a big deal."

"It's okay," I said. "I can pay for my own food."

"No, it's not okay." Amanda turned her whole body toward Cody. "You can never do anything for anyone else. You only take, take, take. It doesn't matter what the person does for you, you never reciprocate."

Here we go again. As if it wasn't already awkward enough.

"I reciprocated," he said.

"Oh, please," she groaned. "We dated for a year, and you couldn't even get me flowers on my birthday or our anniversary. I wanted some big, grand, romantic gesture, but you couldn't even call me back when I asked you to."

"And like you went out of your way for me? I didn't see you doing anything. There were no giant moves on your part."

"Guys don't like big gestures," she said.

"Sure, we do. Right, Wes?"

Wes looked like he did not want to get in the middle of this, but he answered anyway. "I wouldn't complain if someone did one for me."

Amanda sat back in her chair in a huff and folded her arms. I was just happy the conversation was off me, off Jill and how great the new scene was, and off how wonderful Wes and Amanda were together, so I may have stoked the fire just a little. "Like that old eighties movie where the guy stood outside the girl's window with the boom box?"

"Exactly," Wes said.

"Who has a boom box these days?" Amanda said. "I didn't even know what one was until my dad explained it to me."

"The boom box isn't the point," Wes said. "It's that he was willing to put himself out there. He went big."

I couldn't believe Wes knew the movie *Say Anything*. . . .

"I love that kind of thing," I said, "like in *The Notebook*, where he wrote his love a letter every day for a year."

"Or *The Fault in Our Stars*, where he used his wish on his girlfriend," Wes added. "Who wouldn't want something like that? Sure, these examples were all guys making the move, but I think most guys would like to be on the receiving end, too. I know I would."

"Fine, whatever, you win," Amanda said. "Can we go now?"

As nice as it was talking about romantic movies with Wes, Amanda had said the words I had been waiting to hear all night.

I was more than ready for this double date to end. I certainly didn't need to be asked twice.

27

As Amanda and Wes left the restaurant, I hung back.

Amanda didn't bother saying good-bye, but Wes raised his hand in a half wave and gave me a small smile. He looked a little down. Not that I could blame him. He had just witnessed one of the most awkward dates in history, which involved not only his girlfriend but also his girlfriend's ex and the girl who had been crushing on him basically his whole lifetime. And between Cody and Amanda's fight and my soaking myself and the whole table, I'd say it was a disappointing night for all.

"It's not that late," Cody said, and stroked his fingers down my arm. "Want to go hang out at Feiman Park for a bit?"

Was he serious?!! After the date we just had? The answer was a definite no. I had had my fill of Cody for the day. Maybe for the year. "I'm going to stick around here and talk to Kayla a bit," I said. "About tonight," I added, "I think we're probably better off just as friends." And by friends, I really meant friendly acquaintances, as in someone I would say "hi" to in school, but not someone I'd go out of my way to talk to. Flirty, suck-up Emily was dead. This night pounded the final stake into her heart.

He shrugged and mumbled something. I think it was "your loss," but I wasn't positive. As if to punctuate that sentiment, he stopped by the waitress and got her number. Then he smiled at me and raised his hand in some sort of "peace out" sign. "We could have had fun," he said with a wink before walking out.

He was seriously too much. I cringed as I thought back on the evening.

"Em?" Kayla called out.

I grabbed a chair from an empty table and placed it between Kayla and Jace. "I am so happy to finally be crashing your date," I told them.

"Welcome," Jace said.

"All right." I picked an olive off the pizza that sat on their table. "Go ahead. Get it out. Let the jokes begin. I know I did it to myself this time."

"We don't have any jokes," Kayla said.

"Well . . ." Jace interrupted her. "I have a few."

Kayla threw her napkin at him.

"It's okay," I said, covering part of my face with my hands. "You guys can laugh. I probably would be if it happened to someone that wasn't ME." I pointed at their pizza. "Can I?"

Kayla nodded.

Apparently, humiliation made me hungry. "It was bad," I said.

"I know, we saw," Kayla told me.

"You only saw half of it."

Jace stared at me. "Wait. There was more?!"

I took a bite of pizza, then recapped everything they missed: being trapped in the bathroom while Cody flirted with someone else, Amanda and Cody's fighting, my spilling the pop, and the awkwardness with Wes.

"Em, I'm sorry," Kayla said. "I thought your date might have some entertainment value to watch, but I never expected all this."

"It's not your fault. I guess, on the upside, other than the tiny, itty-bitty piece of pride I still had left, there wasn't really anything else for me to lose, right? I'm already the school joke. I couldn't care less about Cody. And it wasn't like Wes ever liked me. Not romantically anyway."

Jace made some sort of weird noise midchew.

"What?" I asked.

"Nothing."

Kayla's eyes zeroed in on him. "What aren't you saying?"

"Nothing," he repeated.

She shook her head. "Ut-uh, you know something. Start talking."

"I don't want to get in the middle of this," he said.

"Middle of what?" I asked.

"Nothing," he said yet again.

Even though his name was short and only one syllable, Kayla managed to drag it out to sound a lot more like three. "Jaaaacccce," she warned, "you already are in the middle. It's too late. So if you know something about Wes that you're not saying, it's time to speak up."

My heart started to beat faster. What did he know? "Please, Jace," I pleaded, "you have to tell me. Please!"

Jace tossed his pizza crust down on his plate. "First, let me get this straight. You like Wes?"

"You know I do. That's why I didn't want to go to the dance."

"I just thought it was because you didn't have a date," he said.

I turned to Kayla. "You never told him?"

"You told me not to, so I didn't. That's what you wanted, right?"

I nodded. "But, Jace," I said, "if you know something, you have to tell me."

He shifted uncomfortably.

"Please," I begged.

He finally relented. "Fine, he may have talked about you."

"What does that mean?"

Jace was really squirming now. "I don't know."

"Yes, you do."

"Okay. It wasn't like we sat around discussing your every move or anything. . . ." His voice trailed off at the end.

"But . . ." I egged him on.

"But he liked you. A lot."

"Why didn't you tell me this before?" Kayla shrieked.

I felt my chest contract. Wes had liked me? I wasn't sure I could still put a sentence together. "Wha, huh, I, when?"

"Jace!" Kayla said.

"He told me not to say anything."

She shook her head. "And you listened?"

He picked up a piece of pizza, but Kayla slapped it out of his hand. "He's my friend," Jace said. "You didn't tell me she liked him. It's the same thing. Besides, he was going to ask her out, but if I told you, you would have told her, and it would have messed everything up."

"Well, you could have said something after you realized he wasn't going to do it anymore," she said.

"Why? She's the one who said she only liked him as a friend."

"What?" I yelled loudly enough that an old couple in the restaurant turned around to stare.

Jace looked confused. "He said you told him you weren't interested."

I slumped down in my chair. "I didn't mean that. Besides, he had already asked Amanda to the dance anyway. He likes her."

"Not really," Jace said.

Kayla squeezed his arm. "Jace, tell us everything he said."

"Amanda asked him to the dance. And she had just gotten out of the hospital. It's kinda harsh to say no to that, but he wanted to take you. He was going to tell you. How could you not know? It was obvious. He was always talking about you, or to you, and driving you around. He still hasn't given me a ride, but he was your personal driver. Me and some of the guys gave him a hard time about it. But then one day he just said you weren't interested, and we didn't bring it up again."

I wasn't interested? I was incredibly interested. I had been since I rode that bike down the driveway when we were little. Maybe even before. This was all my fault. I got jealous over nothing and ran my mouth. If I hadn't said I just saw him as a friend, we'd be together now.

"I blew it. I can't believe he actually liked me."

"Sorry," Jace said.

"And what about now?" Kayla pressed him.

"Huh?" he asked.

She let out an exasperated sigh. "And what are Wes's feelings *now*?"

"What do you think? Who likes to hear the person they like doesn't like them back?"

I was grateful that Kayla was doing the interrogation. I was too overwhelmed to think straight.

"So him and Amanda?" she asked.

"She's been paying a lot of attention to him, and he thought Emily didn't like him, so they've been hanging out. They're not exclusive or anything. But that could change. I mean, she's hot."

Kayla glared at him.

"Not as hot as you," he corrected himself.

But her eyes were still bugged out, and she nodded just a millimeter in my direction. "Or you, Emily," he added.

I knew he was just saying that to appease Kayla, but it didn't matter what Jace thought about me, it mattered what Wes thought.

I needed to fix this. Wes needed to know the truth. He needed to know I liked him. Even if he didn't feel the same way back anymore. It was a chance I had to take.

28

The next day after school, Jill and Kayla came over for a get-Wes-back strategy session. We sat around my dining room table to brainstorm.

"I really messed up," I said, "but I'm going to fix it. I just need something big. Wes said he liked grand gestures, so I'm going to give him one. *If* I can figure out what to do. I can't blow this. It has to be thought out. I can't just be impulsive and mess everything up. I need to show him that I took the time to do something special because he's worth it to me. That it's him I always liked, not Cody. So any ideas would be greatly appreciated."

"Didn't you guys talk about that *Say Anything* . . . movie? Get a boom box and go to his house," Jill suggested.

"I'm never going to find one of those."

"Then maybe just throw rocks at his window and hold a sign up?" Kayla offered, and unwrapped a Hershey's Kiss. The table was covered with candy. I was hoping a sugar rush would inspire some good ideas.

"My luck, I'd get the wrong room and break his brother's window, and his mom would call the cops."

"Fair point," Jill said.

"You can fill his locker with something. Roses or balloons or love notes or"—Kayla popped another candy into her mouth—"chocolate Kisses?"

"She'd need his combo."

"And if the Kisses melted," I said, "I'd just cause him problems."

Kayla tugged at her ponytail. "Okay. How about something personal to the two of you, a fun moment or something you shared."

"He always gives you rides. You can borrow my car if you want to drive him somewhere," Jill said.

That was supersweet of her to offer, but I was going to be too nervous to be behind the wheel of a motor vehicle. "Maybe something that doesn't involve machinery."

Kayla jumped up. "Your grocery cart. Do something with that."

"What? Offer to push him around all day while I recite bad Shakespeare sonnets to him?"

"That's it," Jill said.

I looked at her like she was nuts. "I was kidding."

"I don't mean that exactly. I mean Wes and Amanda are performing the *Romeo and Juliet* scene tomorrow. Maybe it should be Romeo and . . . Emily instead?"

"I cannot go back out there again. The definite humiliation, the probable suspension, and there's no way I can ruin your scene again."

"You forget," she said. "It's not *my* scene anymore. You told me what Amanda said. I had even offered to do a few catch-up rehearsals for her. She totally lied and told me it wasn't necessary, that she remembered everything. She didn't even mention Ryan. I was going to get to the auditorium tomorrow totally expecting to see my scene. Can you imagine how Ryan would have jumped on that?"

What Amanda did to Jill still made me angry.

"So you definitely wouldn't be ruining anything for *me*," Jill continued. "But Amanda would get to see what it feels like to be replaced last second without being told. Plus, I have a feeling your version of *Romeo and Juliet* will be a lot more entertaining than anything I—or Ryan—could have come up with."

"And," Kayla added, "you keep saying you want to go big. This would definitely qualify."

I shook my head. "It's tempting, but I don't know if I want to go THAT big. Besides, I wouldn't even know what to do once I got up there."

"Maybe you just need a director," Jill said, and nodded toward Kayla. "Or two."

"Yeah?" I asked.

"Yeah," she repeated. "You helped me with Seth, now I can return the favor." She got extra shy whenever she mentioned his name, especially after what happened at the dance. I caught her kissing him in the corner of the cafeteria, but I wasn't the only one. Mr. Asghar, the chemistry teacher, saw them, too, and asked them if he needed to get out the hose to break them apart. Jill was mortified. Seth had been pretty embarrassed, too. They were both big blushers and were stop-sign red when I caught up with them afterward. It was so noticeable that Kayla couldn't keep herself from secretly taking a picture of them. If they were still a couple next year (which I was definitely rooting for), she planned to print it up and give it to them as an anniversary gift.

"I didn't fix you up for something in return."

"I know, but that doesn't mean I still don't want to help you."

"We both want to," Kayla said. "And, seriously, this sounds like fun. Trying to top your last turn as Juliet? This will be insane. The grandest of grand gestures."

"But the three of us can do it," Jill assured me.

I hoped she was right, because I was going all-in.

I pulled out a notebook, and we got busy planning.

Come tomorrow, Emily Stein was going to reclaim her role— and her Romeo!

29

This was crazy. There was no way I could go through with this plan. There were smarter ways to tell Wes I cared. It wasn't too late to back out. That lump in the back of my throat all day told me I probably should. Last period was just minutes away. I had to make up my mind. Kayla and Jill were about to set everything in motion. I watched the clock tick closer to do-or-die time. Four minutes. Three. Two. One. The bell rang.

This was it. Against my better judgment, I raced to the auditorium. I was supposed to go to English first, and we were going to walk to the performance as a class, but I needed every extra second I could get. Wes, Amanda, Kayla, and Jill were already there. They got special permission to go early since they were a part of the show. Wes and Amanda were obviously the actors. Kayla was helping them get into costume. And Jill, well, even though Amanda didn't think of her as the director anymore, Mrs. Heller did. So we decided to use that to our advantage. Jill was in charge of keeping everyone where they needed to be—including my teacher. And Kayla had just as tricky a task.

"Ready?" Jill asked when I reached her.

"Not really."

She put a hand on each of my arms and gave me a performance pep talk. "You can do this. We rehearsed. You know this. Now you just need to go out there, have fun, and win over Romeo." I must not have looked persuaded, because her voice took on that determined tone it always does when she was superserious. "Wes Rosenthal has been the only thing you've talked about for weeks. Months. Years. If you don't do this, how are you going to feel? Especially if he winds up with Amanda. I know you. You're going to regret it if you don't try. So, psych yourself up. You are ready. Okay?"

"Okay."

"Good, Kayla should have your costume in a minute."

I nodded, but I still wasn't 100 percent convinced. Jill made really great points, but this was *so* over the top. As we stood there in silence, waiting, my thoughts became deafening. *This was going to be the dumbest move of my lifetime.* Who hijacked the spotlight and made a huge spectacle of themselves—intentionally?

I started pacing. *Go take a seat in the auditorium, Emily.* It wasn't too late. That was the smart thing. The rational thing. Right?

"Watch the . . ." Jill yelled, her voice tapering off as the door to dressing room one swung open, knocking me flat on my butt.

"Emily, are you okay?"

It was Wes. Of course it was.

He crouched down next me. "I'm so sorry. I should have been more careful," he said, giving me his arm to help me up.

"Hiiii," I sputtered, ungracefully getting to my feet while

smoothing down my skirt. At least I didn't flash him. "It's fine. It was my fault. Wasn't watching where I was going."

"What are you doing back here?"

"Never know when you'll need an understudy, right?"

"Wouldn't want anyone else," he said, and smiled at me. And I remembered why I was doing this. For Wes, the guy who gave me my first Valentine when we were five, the one who picked me up when I fell, the one who still smiled at me and said nice things even though I hurt him. There was no changing my mind or backing out now. Nerves or not, I needed him to know just how much he meant to me. He deserved a grand gesture.

Kayla opened the door to dressing room two and quickly shut it behind her when she saw all of us. Her arms were filled with fabric.

"Wes," Jill said, ushering him away. "I was thinking it would be better if you entered from the other side. It will be more powerful if you don't see Juliet until you're on stage. Once I introduce the scene, that will be your cue to enter."

Once Wes was out of sight, Kayla dumped everything she was holding in his dressing room. "Okay," she said. "We don't have much time. Amanda thinks I'm steaming out some giant wrinkle in the back of the gown. We need to get moving before she gets suspicious."

Kayla was right. Even though part of me was still panicking, I pushed the feeling aside. I had work to do. I grabbed the doorstop I had stashed in my backpack last night and wedged it under Amanda's door. She'd be trapped, at least temporarily. Jill came back, and the three of us grabbed the giant tree-stump prop that had been used in one of the other scenes and pushed it up against the door as an extra precaution.

"This thing weighs a ton," Kayla said.

"That's the point," Jill informed her.

"Are you sure the key won't work?" she asked.

"Yes," Jill said as we finally maneuvered the stump exactly where it needed to be. Jill had informed us that even when you locked a door you could still get out from the inside. Otherwise, it was a fire-code violation.

"Kayla?" Amanda called out. We apparently hadn't been as quiet as we had hoped.

"She'll just be another minute," Jill answered for her. "Don't worry, it's not like we can do this without you." She turned back to us. "She's not the only one who can lie. Now go get dressed."

Kayla and I rushed into the other dressing room, where she had dumped the costume. There were a pair of jeans, a T-shirt, a bra, and a sweater there, too. "What is all this?" I asked.

"Well, I figured, even if Amanda managed to get the door open, it's not like she's going to run out practically naked."

"Kayla! You stole her clothes?"

"What? You say that like locking her in a dressing room is that much better. I'm going to give them back to her after. This will just ensure you more time. Now come on, put the gown on."

Yeah, this was all definitely insane.

I slipped the dress on and sucked in my breath as Kayla tied the ribbons.

There was banging on the other dressing room door. "What is going on out there? Why can't I get out?" Amanda yelled.

Jill popped her head into my dressing room. "I think we should get started. ASAP."

"Good call," I said.

"Get me out of here," Amanda screamed. I prayed no one heard her.

I walked over to her dressing room. "I'm sorry," I called to her. "I have to do this. I just need five minutes max. I promise we'll let you out after that. Then you can do your scene. It will be a win-win for everyone."

"Emily, open this door," she seethed. "I swear, you are all going to pay as soon as I get out of here."

I didn't doubt that one bit. But it wasn't like I was stealing her moment altogether. She was still going to get to perform afterward. I wasn't going to be on stage forever. Still, I felt a twinge of guilt, but then I reminded myself what she did to Jill, and I pushed it aside. This was for love. I couldn't worry about anything else—especially not Amanda—right now.

Jill took the stage, and I waited on the sideline to make my entrance. Amanda was still loudly trying to get out. She had a decent set of lungs on her, but hopefully the acoustics would make it hard to hear her from the auditorium.

"Welcome, everyone," Jill began as Kayla did a final check-in with me.

"Do you have your paper?"

"Yep, and my phone."

"Perfect, now go crush it," she said.

"Without further ado," Jill concluded, "please enjoy this unique take on *Romeo and* . . ." She paused. ". . . *Juliet*."

She left the stage.

This was it. It was time for the most important performance of my life.

30

I was really doing this. Mustering all of my courage, I dashed onto the stage. The audience wasn't helping my nerves. I could almost feel an excited energy permeate the room as I stepped up onto the balcony.

"Here we go again," one person called out. "This is going to be good," another said. I looked out at the crowd. Huge mistake. Not only could I see Jill trying to buy me some time by talking to Mrs. Heller, but about ten phones were raised in the air waiting to catch my latest humiliation. Although I guess I couldn't blame anyone, I brought this on myself.

I just hoped Wes would find this endearing and not mortifying. Laughter and jokes from my classmates I could take, but rejection from Wes was going to be a lot harder.

But I had to be brave. Risks could pay off. And even if they didn't, they were a lot better than living with the "what ifs."

It was now or never. I smiled at Wes and pulled a piece of paper out from my dress pocket (I knew better than to think I could recite anything from memory when I was nervous) and started to read.

"I know you must be wondering why I'm here, oh my

Wes-eo, Wes-eo . . ." My voice was shaking. I hoped what sounded cute while sitting around a table with my two best friends didn't come off as pathetically cheesy on stage. But I had to keep going. I was the one who always said Shakespeare didn't make any sense, that anyone could write gibberish like that. Well, now it was my turn. (Which, FYI, totally gave me a new appreciation for Shakespeare's stuff.) And while my words might not have been pure poetry, or any type of poetry for that matter (I was definitely more of a math and science girl), I tried, I was making the effort, and hopefully that counted for something. I forged ahead. "It's because I had to repair-eth my giant mess-eo."

I glanced up at him. His mouth was slightly open. I didn't know if that was a good or bad sign, but I wasn't going to let that stop me. I just kept on reading. "I jumped to conclusions when I thought you were saying no, so I'm trying to fix-eth that right now with this show. I wasn't brave enough to tell you how I genuinely felt, that when I see you, my heart starts to melt." I was dying to see his face, to see how he was responding, but I couldn't look up again. Not yet. I needed to get through this, and, well, I was too afraid to see what he thought. I kept reading. "I really wanted to go with you to the dance-eth, so I truly hope you'll give me a second chance-eth."

I pulled out my phone from the hidden pocket in the dress. It was charged this time. I pressed my thumb on the screen to turn it on, and up popped the song I had ready to go. This was it. I took a deep breath (as deep as I could while wearing a corset), steadied my hand, hit Play, and held the phone up over my head. The song "In Your Eyes" from *Say Anything* . . . blasted from the speaker.

Please like this, please like this, please like this, I silently pleaded.

I knew the entire auditorium was watching me, but somehow it felt as if it were just Wes and me. His eyes were the only ones that mattered. I braved a look. His face was softer than before. He still looked utterly shocked, but it seemed like I was getting through to him. I just had one more line to go. I could do this. "I did this grand——"

A loud crash pulled me from the moment and turned my attention to the back of the auditorium.

The doors had been slammed open, sending them flying into the wall. And standing smack in the middle of the opening was a livid Amanda.

She was wearing a costume that had been left in the dressing room. A poofy bright pink ball gown from the senior class's production of *The Wizard of Oz*. It was about four sizes too big for her. She was holding it up with one hand and pointing at me with the other. Her hair was a mess, her eyes wild, and her teeth bared. Basically, she looked like Glinda the Good Witch, if Glinda had fought off the zombie apocalypse and lost.

"Oh no," I said.

"GET OFF MY STAGE!" she screamed, and barreled down the aisle. I had always heard the expression, *if looks could kill*, but I never truly experienced it until that moment. She ran onto the stage, and I was no fool; as she headed for me, I went the other direction.

Normally she'd be faster than me—which is not saying much, since I came in dead last in the high school fitness exam, but I had the upper hand at the moment. Even though we were both in gowns, hers had so much mesh underneath the bell skirt she was about six feet in circumference. Not to mention, if she didn't hold up the dress, either it would fall off her or she'd trip over the bottom. Still, she was determined, which meant I had to do something. I wasn't ready to leave the stage. Not yet. I hadn't finished what I had set out to do. "Well, um, it looks like Rosaline has returned-th, and she is pissed-eth," I said as I raced behind Wes for cover.

Rosaline was Romeo's ex, and if I had my way, Amanda would soon be Wes's.

"I am Juliet," Amanda spat as she stood in front of Wes, trying to figure out how to get to me.

"What's in a name?" I said. I was pretty sure that was a line from the original scene. "Doff thy name."

"Emily," she said. "I'm serious. Get out of here."

"I will, I promise. I just have a little more to read. Just let me get it out, and I'll go. I'll never bother you again."

"Are you kidding me?" she growled. "You locked me in the dressing room and stole my clothes. I had to climb out the window, and now you want me to let you finish?"

"If you wouldn't mind."

She didn't appreciate my humor. "You are so dead."

This wasn't good. "It appear-eth that she's gone mad-eth, huh, Romeo? Get thee to a nunnery," I proclaimed.

"Wrong play. That's *Hamlet*," Amanda said, and lunged to the right. I moved at the same time. Now I was in front of Wes and she was behind him, but I could tell she was ready to pounce again.

Wes hadn't said a word. I think he might have been in a slight state of shock. His eyes were open crazy wide, like when you're watching a TV show and your favorite character gets offed out of nowhere. It was that kind of OMG stunned. Not that I could blame him. Wes was basically serving as a shield as the Pepto-Bismol Princess tried to take down his jilted Juliet— all while eighties music played in the background. I had been too busy dodging Amanda to turn it off.

"I can't believe you did this to me," she yelled, and this time moved to the left.

I was ready for her. I started running. "It wasn't *to* you. It wasn't even about you. It was about me."

"Exactly," Amanda said, and reached out to grab me. I just got away. "You didn't think about anyone but yourself. This was supposed to be *my* moment."

I wanted to point out that that was just as selfish, but it didn't seem like the right time.

"I'm sorry," I said. "But I needed something big. A grand gesture."

Wes's eyebrows scrunched together ever so slightly. "That's what this is about?" he asked.

I nodded, and in that one second pause, Amanda managed to grab my arm. "It's time for you to say good-bye-eth," she said, and pulled me toward stage right.

But I wasn't ready. I needed to see what Wes thought. I pulled away and ran back to him. Amanda was right on my tail. She lunged. She hit her target, and we both tumbled to the ground.

"Enough," a voice called out. It was Mrs. Heller. I was kind of surprised it took her this long to stop me. Jill had done a good job stalling her. Although Mrs. Heller was probably just as stunned watching this train wreck as the rest of the audience. She had probably been frozen in disbelief. "Emily," she said, "get over here now."

I knew I was facing detention, suspension, or even worse. And buckets full of humiliation. But I came too far to not finish what I started.

A grand gesture was supposed to be grand. Not a cop-out. Not stop when you get scared.

I wasn't going to turn into a "what if" story. It was time to risk it all.

I ignored my teacher. I ignored Amanda. I ignored the crowd. I ignored everyone but my Romeo.

I pushed Amanda off me and stood up. Wes was just watching me. He wasn't frowning or smiling or anything. This was it. I pulled out my paper and read my last line. "I did this grand gesture-eth for you and the school to see, because you've always been-eth the one for me."

Please let this have worked. "Wes," I said, dropping my silly rhymes and my Shakespeare accent. "It's—"

"Emily!" This time Mrs. Heller was standing behind me. "Principal's office this instant."

I turned to face her. "I—"

"I don't want to hear it. Let's go," she said, and escorted me off the stage. I turned to see Wes's reaction, but Amanda blocked my view.

I had no clue what he was thinking. Had I blown everything? There was no way to know. Not now anyway.

It was time to face my punishment.

I just hoped it was all worth it.

31

Detention was torture, and not because it was detention, but because I had no idea what Wes was thinking. And it just gave me time to sit there and replay the whole awful thing over and over again. Why hadn't he said anything? I told him how much I liked him, and he just stood there gawking at me. Was he processing? Or did he not know how to tell me that he didn't feel the same way anymore? That had to be it. If he had wanted me, he would have done something—chased after me, screamed out, pulled out his phone and played a song. But he didn't.

I put my head down on my desk. I was so sure the grand gesture was a good idea. How could I have been so wrong? I hadn't even had a chance to talk to Jill or Kayla. After the principal's office, it was straight to detention. At least they let me change into my regular clothes. It was one less reminder of how stupid I had been.

"Hey," some sophomore sitting in front of me said. I looked up, and he was holding his phone up, just inches from my face. "This you?"

I slammed my face back down. My new humiliation was

already up on the World Wide Web for me and everyone else to relive.

"There's a bunch of 'em posted," he continued, ignoring the fact that I clearly did not want to talk. Where was the teacher to tell everyone to be quiet when I needed her? "You got a ton of hits already."

I didn't even want to know which parts of my embarrassing display were uploaded. Where I began reciting my ridiculous poem? Where Amanda tackled me? Where I declared my undying love, only to be met with a blank stare? All of them were cringe-worthy. Why hadn't Heller demanded the principal suspend me? Then I could have spent the next few days at home, away from Wes, Amanda, everyone. But no, she cut me a break, because I was usually such a "well-behaved student" (other than my constant talking in class). Although, honestly, I think it was because she felt sorry for me. There I was, putting myself out there, following in the footsteps of literary and movie greats who took risks and declared their undying love, only to be royally rejected.

The sophomore finally turned back around in his seat, and I spent the rest of my detention trying to wish away the day.

"Are you free?" Kayla asked, peeking into the classroom after everyone filed out. Jill was right behind her.

"Yeah, for today anyway. Thanks for waiting."

Jill dropped into the seat next to me. "We wouldn't leave you here. Not after what you went through today. How long did you get?"

"Today, next week, and the one after."

"Ouch," she said. "It could have been worse, I guess."

"We feel guilty," Kayla said. "We should be in here with you. We pushed you to do this."

"No," I objected. "This is not on you. I made this mess. I told Heller it was all me, that you guys had no idea what was going on, and I want to keep it that way."

"It doesn't seem fair," Jill said.

"Life isn't fair," I answered, and shoved my books into my bag. If it was, it wouldn't always be the people like Amanda who got the guy. "Have you seen Wes?"

They shook their heads.

"Not since the scene," Kayla said.

"So they did it?" I asked. "After I left?"

"Yeah," Jill answered, her voice soft.

"How was it? How was Amanda?"

Kayla put her hand on my arm. "She was no you."

"So you mean she was amazing then?" My little stunt probably wound up pushing her even closer to Wes. I could picture the two of them laughing over the mess I created.

Jill stood up. "You know what, let's get out of here. We can pick up some ice cream and watch a movie. Sound good?"

I knew they were trying to make me feel better, and I appreciated it, but I just needed some time alone. I'd liked Wes for so long, but I blew it. It was over. Accepting that was hard, but I had to start. "Can I just have a few minutes?"

"Of course," Jill said. "We'll wait for you by my car."

Once they left, I sunk my face into my hands. Why couldn't anything ever go my way? I tried to hold back my tears, but it wasn't working. I needed to snap out of it. I had nothing to be ashamed of or upset over. Even though today didn't work out, I did my best, I tried, and that was something. Wes was just some guy. A guy who didn't want me. It was stupid to cry over him. I had other things in my life. So what if a broken heart was one of them?

I just sat there, head down in silence for a moment.

But something changed. I could feel someone standing over me. Had Jill and Kayla come back?

I looked up.

It was Wes.

32

"Hi," Wes said, taking the seat next to me.

"Hi." I looked up, and over Wes's shoulder I saw Jill and Kayla peering in through the doorway. They were giving me big thumbs-up signs. They must have crossed paths with Wes in the hallway and come back to spy. I bugged my eyes out at them to go; and after making a few excited faces and mouthing "OMG" and "this is good," they waved and left.

Were they right? Was this good? Or was Wes just being a nice guy and coming by to let me down gently and to say "let's be friends"? I wasn't sure what to do, so I waited for him to start talking.

"You okay?" he asked.

There was no hiding that I'd been crying, but I rubbed my eyes with my sleeve anyway. "It's been a long day." I didn't know what to feel. Why was he here? I was so confused, and having him so close was twisting up all my emotions. A fresh tear made its way down my cheek. Wes wiped it away with his finger.

He needed to stop doing things like that now. Unless he was

here to tell me he liked me. Because it was all those tiny acts he did that made me fall for him totally and completely.

Part of me just wanted to yell, *Tell me why you're here already. Spit it out.* But I held back. I had already made a spectacle of myself today. Whatever Wes had to say—good or bad—I was just going to listen.

"About what you said out there," he said.

"Yeah?" I asked.

"Did you mean it?"

There was the teensiest, tiniest part of me that wanted to say no, to protect myself, in case he didn't feel the same way, but that's what got me into trouble the first time. So I went for the truth.

"Yes. I meant all of it. Every word." My breathing had picked up. Amanda may have been right. I did sound kind of Darth Vader–ish. But I couldn't help it, I was supernervous.

"Is this just because it didn't work out with Cody?" he asked. "Because he got back together with Amanda last night?"

"He what? I thought Amanda was into you?"

He didn't answer. He was just watching me. Wait. He couldn't possibly think I made a fool of myself in front of the whole school because I was upset about Cody?

"You know I never really liked him, right? It was never about him." I laid it all out. "When I found out you were going to the dance with Amanda, I was upset, so I tried to make you jealous. I know it was dumb."

"It worked," he said quietly. "You know, you were the one I wanted to go to the dance with."

I looked down at my hands. "But you took Amanda."

"She asked, and she had just gotten out of the hospital. I didn't know how to say no. I should have, though."

"So you're not into her?"

"Never was."

He put his fingers lightly on my chin and lifted my face back up so I was looking at him. "I was going to tell you, but then you said those things about just being friends."

"That was because I just found out you were taking out someone else. Someone who was hanging all over you."

"I thought that might have been why, but when I tried to talk to you about it, you were all about Cody, so I backed off."

Of course he did, because he was a good guy.

"I'm sorry I didn't listen. It's just that Amanda was always there. Even before she went into the hospital. I thought it was something more."

"She kept coming around, and texting, and I don't know. It wasn't anything real. Apparently, I'm the guy everyone uses to make Cody jealous."

"I never cared what Cody thought." I squeezed my eyes shut so I wouldn't have to look at him when I admitted this. "I only cared about you. And it made me do stupid things. I wasn't thinking straight. I just liked you so much. I still do. Like you, that is."

"Good," he said, and put his hand on my arm, "because I like you, too."

Was I dreaming? I opened one eye. "Even after today?"

He smiled. It was one of those big ones that made his eyes sparkle and showed off his dimple. "Especially after today."

I couldn't help but smile back. "I guess my grand gesture worked."

"I guess it did. Although, I would have still liked you without it. Not that I didn't love your rhyming."

I cringed slightly as I thought about my poem. Wes-eo and mess-eo. Dance-eth and chance-eth. I really needed to stick to math. "I know it was cheesy and corny. English and Shakespeare are not my subjects."

"I thought it was perfect."

"You did?"

"I did."

He was looking at me so intently I felt light-headed. All that disappointment and regret I had been feeling not even half an hour ago had been replaced with dizzying happiness. Wes wanted me! It was really happening.

"Well, I . . ." I stopped speaking when he stood up. My eyes followed him as he moved closer. The next thing I knew, Wes was mere inches away from me. I felt my heartbeat quicken and my body move toward his. This was it! Wes's hands cupped my face, and then slowly, tenderly, his lips pressed against mine.

Wes Rosenthal was kissing me!

When he pulled away, I wasn't sure I could even remember my name.

He locked eyes with mine. "I don't have a poem," he said, "but you've always been the one for me. You were my first crush. You were the girl down the street I always wanted to hang out with. Emily, you're my Juliet."

We held each other's gaze, and then he leaned in toward me again, never once breaking eye contact. All I could think about was the taste of his mouth. When I didn't think I could take it even a second longer, his lips were back on mine. The years of dreaming about this moment didn't even come close to the real thing. It was the perfect kiss. A sweet, passionate, hot, Romeo and Juliet kiss.

And just like that, my tragedy turned-eth into a love story-eth.

ACKNOWLEDGMENTS

I AM CONSTANTLY IN AWE OF ALL the incredible people at Swoon Reads and Macmillan. Thank you for helping me bring this book to life. I feel very lucky to have you in my corner.

Jean Feiwel, thank you for believing in me. It's an honor to have you as my publisher.

Editor extraordinaire Holly West, thank you, thank you, thank you! This book is so much better because of you. You are amazing, and I've loved working with you!

Lauren Scobell, I don't even know where to start. *Romeo & What's Her Name* would probably still be sitting in a file waiting to be finished if it wasn't for you. Not only are you an incredible friend, but you are one of the most talented, hardworking people I know. Thank you for everything.

My main character isn't the only Emily to play a role in this book. Emily Settle and Emily Petrick, thank you for all your help, feedback, and more!

To Jonathan Yaged, president of Macmillan Children's Publishing Group, Rebecca Syracuse, who designed the amazing cover, Holly Hunnicutt and everyone in sub rights, Caitlin Sweeny, Caitlin Crocker, Kallam McKay and everyone in digital, Kathryn Little, Ashley Woodfolk and everyone in marketing, Allison Verost and the whole publicity team, Mariel Dawson and the advertising team, production editor Melinda Ackell, copy editor Tracy Koontz, and everyone else involved in this book, I am so grateful for all your help and support. Thank you for everything.

To the Swoon community, you are fantastic. Thank you for your input, your thoughts, and your kind words. I truly appreciate it.

The librarians, booksellers, bloggers, reviewers, and readers, thank you for spending some of your time with Emily and her friends. It means a lot.

To Fox 5 and all my current and former colleagues. You are such a supportive group of people. Thank you for being there for me.

A big part of this book is about friendship, and I feel very lucky to have amazing friends. From the ones I've known forever to the ones who've recently entered my life, from the coworkers to the cousins, and to everyone in between—thank you. Your support, your encouragement, and your love mean the world to me.

(And special shout-out to Anna Hecker Schumacher and Judy Goldschmidt, who not only looked over the short story version of *Romeo & What's Her Name* but made amazing suggestions that made it from rough draft to final version of the book. Thank you for your feedback and friendship. And a thank-you to the group of authors I first debuted alongside of that encouraged me to write the short story. You are indeed a talented group of people.)

To my extended and immediate family, I adore you. Mom, Jordan, Andrea, Liam, and Alice, you do more for me than you could ever know. You are the world to me. I love you and am so thankful for you. To my father, whose love for books was only second to his love for his family, I know you are looking down and smiling. I love you.

And, of course, I can't leave out my first crush, the one who later gave me rides in high school, tried to show me how to drive a stick-shift car, and made me so nervous (in a good way) that I hid under the table from him at the dance. Thank you for the memories. You will always hold a soft spot in my heart.

FEELING BOOKISH?

Turn the page for some

Swoonworthy **EXTRAS**

EMILY'S FAILED ATTEMPTS AT POETRY FOR WES

"Okay," Jill said. "If you're going to go up on stage to win over Wes, we have to have something for you to say."

"Ooooh." Kayla perked up and leaned forward in her chair. "What if you actually memorized the words to the *Romeo and Juliet* scene and performed it perfectly?"

"I'm afraid I'd screw it up again."

"You wouldn't," she assured me.

"*But* Mrs. Heller *would* probably cut her off before she got very far." Jill was always the voice of reason. "You need something short and to the point but also romantic."

Kayla jumped up. "A poem. You can read him a sonnet. Or better yet, you can write something yourself!"

I actually snorted. Me? Write a poem? She couldn't be serious. Only she was.

"It will be so sweet. Who doesn't want something written especially for them?"

Jill nodded. "That's perfect."

"Yeah, perfect until he hears my pathetic attempt and runs the other direction. What am I going to write?" I asked, and began to improvise.

"Wes. *W* is for how wonderful you are. *E* is for the emotions you make me feel. *S* is for *short*—as in, I'm grateful your name is short, because I suck at poetry."

"You might want to keep working," Jill said.

"No kidding!" I said, and stuffed a piece of chocolate in my mouth. This was ridiculous.

"Try rhyming," Kayla offered.

"Poems don't have to rhyme," Jill informed her.

"I know that." Kayla scrunched up her face. "But you just heard her free verse."

"Point taken."

"Ha-ha," I said, and threw chocolate Kisses at them. I wasn't about to tell them that I didn't even know what *free verse* meant—although from the context I guessed it meant something that didn't rhyme. I was *so* not a poetry girl. Couldn't I just help Wes with his computer? That would be so much easier. But I knew I had to get out of my comfort zone. I was supposed to be doing something grand, not simple. "Okay, I'll try rhyming." What rhymed with *Wes? Less, Loch Ness, dress* . . . I took a few minutes to jot something on paper.

"Well, let's hear it," Jill said when I put the pencil down.

I covered my face with my hands. "It's pitifully embarrassing. Seriously. It's worse than me humming on stage and getting a book pummeled at my head."

"Then we definitely have to hear this," Kayla said.

"Okay," I relented, "but don't say you weren't warned. I don't want to get sued when your ears start bleeding."

"I'm sure it's not that bad," Jill said.

"*I* wouldn't be," I told her. "Here it goes." I couldn't believe

I was going to read this out loud. At least I'd give my friends a laugh. But Jill and Kayla were one thing—how was I ever going to do this in front of my classmates? And Wes? I clutched my paper, cleared my throat, and started reading in my best announcer voice.

"Wes, I have something to confess, so here I am to profess how much I want to feel your caress. I guess what I'm trying to stress is that I obsess over whether you will say yes. Nevertheless, here I am without much finesse, trying to assess what you think of my little address." I wasn't sure I could even get out the last line with a straight face. There was a reason I didn't write things. "Please say this was a success, oh, my Wes, Wes, Wes."

I cringed as I looked up at them. "Well?" I could see they were both trying really, really hard to hold back their laughter. Jill's face was red, and Kayla looked like she was about to have tears come streaming down.

I couldn't help but laugh at their expressions, which opened the floodgates. Pretty soon we were all doubled over in hysterics.

"You know," Jill said, "not everything has to rhyme with *Wes*. You can have some variety. But I like your pro-*cess*."

"Yeah," Kayla added, trying to get out words through her laughter, "it's a work in pro-*gress*."

"More like a *mess*," I joined in.

"Nah," Jill said, "you managed to *impress*."

"Wait, wait, wait," Kayla said. "I've got a line for you. Wes, I have to *stress* how much I want to see you in various states of *undress*."

Swoon READS

"Shh," I warned. "My parents are downstairs. You want them to flip out?" But that didn't stop them.

Kayla threw a chocolate Kiss from earlier back at me. "You were the one who used *caress* and *obsess*."

"Only because they rhymed and I couldn't think of anything else!"

"How about this?" Jill chimed in. "Oh, Wes, you *luminesce*. 'You'll be the prince and I'll be the *princess*.'"

"Hey, that last part was Taylor Swift," I objected. "Mine would have sounded a lot better if I could have just used her lyrics!"

"Okay, I *acquiesce*," she said, "but we di-*gress* with our chatti-*ness*. Let's get down to busi-*ness*."

She was right. I needed to get this done—to let Wes know how I felt, even if it was under slight duress.

I had no choice; it was time to find my voice.

For never was a story of more woe than crushing on a boy who doesn't know.

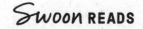

A COFFEE DATE

between author Shani Petroff and her editor, Holly West

GETTING TO KNOW YOU

HW: Do you have an OTP, a favorite fictional couple?
SP: There are so many amazing fictional couples, but in ode to the Shakespeare references in this book, I'll go with one from the Bard's plays—Hermia and Lysander from *A Midsummer Night's Dream*—but before the magic messes everything up! Fortunately, all's well that ends well and everything turns out the way it's supposed to for them! (I've always wanted to play Hermia on stage—it seems like such a fun part!)

HW: I was one of the Mechanicals in our college production of *A Midsummer Night's Dream* and will always have a fondness for that play. ☺ Do you have any hobbies? Other than writing, of course. Writing doesn't count as a hobby when you are a published author.
SP: I've always loved acting and improv and try to do it whenever I can. My schedule has been insanely busy lately, so I haven't been able to do it as much as I would like. Most of my free time is spent writing, volunteering for a nonprofit that I

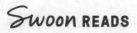

support, hanging out with family and friends, binge-watching my favorite TV shows, and having romantic (mis)adventures!

HW: And my favorite question—if you were a superhero, what would your superpower be?
SP: I've actually had long conversations about this! And after much debate, I decided that if I could pick any power it would be the power of persuasion. Want to get into the evil professor's secret lab? No problem—someone will open the door right up for you. Want to be invisible? Just tell everyone they can't see you and poof! Done. World peace? A couple of sound bites on TV, and we're well on our way. There's so much good you can do with it!

THE SWOON READS EXPERIENCE

HW: How did you first learn about Swoon Reads?
SP: Through the director of Swoon Reads, the lovely and talented Lauren Scobell. She had been talking about it and posted information on Twitter and Facebook.

HW: What made you decide to post your manuscript?
SP: I've always loved romantic comedies, and I had a short story that I wanted to turn into a full-length book. So after hearing really great things about Swoon Reads from Lauren and others, I decided to go for it!

HW: What was your experience like on the site before you were chosen?

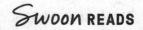

SP: As it got closer to decision day, I was constantly logging on, reading comments, hitting refresh, and seeing what people thought of my work. It was a nail-biter but also exciting!

HW: **Once you were chosen, who was the first person you told, and how did you celebrate?**
SP: First, I called my crush at the time, but I got his voice mail, so I called my brother to celebrate! I also thought I told my mom, but she insists I didn't. Oops!

THE WRITING LIFE

HW: **When did you realize you wanted to be a writer?**
SP: I've always loved books and writing and thought I'd write something "someday." And then several years back I decided it was time to get serious, and I made finishing a book a priority.

HW: **Do you have any writing rituals?**
SP: No rituals, but meeting deadlines is very important to me. So even though I procrastinate from time to time, when that due date approaches, I do what it takes to make sure it's met.

HW: **Where did the idea for *Romeo & What's Her Name* start?**
SP: The original idea was sparked from an incredibly embarrassing moment I experienced in high school. I had to recite a poem in French for a contest, but I didn't give myself enough time to memorize the words. (I thought I'd be able to do it during the bus ride—boy was I wrong!) But I got up there and

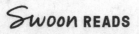

tried anyway. I basically spoke in gibberish with a bad French accent. I still cringe (and laugh) when I think back on it.

HW: At least you were brave enough to try! I think I would have chickened out. Do you ever get writer's block? How do you get back on track?
SP: I definitely have moments when I'm at a loss. To get back on track, I have to force myself to sit down and just write. I tell myself it doesn't have to be my best work—I just need to get something down, and then I can go back and fix it later. Deadlines also get me moving. I work well under pressure and that sense of urgency kicks me into gear.

HW: What's the best writing advice you've ever heard?
SP: The one that sticks out to me right now is from Stephen King: "If you want to be a writer, you must do two things above all others: read a lot and write a lot. There's no way around these two things that I'm aware of, no shortcut."

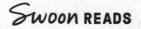

ROMEO &
WHAT'S HER NAME

DISCUSSION QUESTIONS

1. Emily is forced to go on stage unprepared and forgets her lines. Have you ever been unprepared for something like that? How did you handle it?

2. Emily's friendships with Jill and Kayla play a big role throughout this book. What does being a good friend mean to you? What's the craziest thing you've ever done for your friend?

3. Amanda was constantly picking on Emily. What would you do if you had been in Emily's shoes?

4. Why do you think Amanda behaved the way she did?

5. Wes's brother was having a hard time fitting in. If you went to school with him, how would you help him out?

6. Emily encountered some very embarrassing situations. Do you think she handled them well? What would you have done differently?

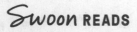

7. Emily eventually began to warm up to Shakespeare. How do you feel about his plays?

8. Besides (spoiler alert) going back on stage, what else could Emily have done to let Wes know she genuinely cared?

9. What are your favorite grand gestures—in literature and in real life?

10. A rhyming couplet is a pair of lines that not only rhyme and have the same meter but also complete a thought. Shakespeare's *Romeo and Juliet* ends with this one:

   For never was a story of more woe
   Than this of Juliet and her Romeo.

   To describe *Romeo & What's Her Name*, we have been using this rhyming couplet:

   For never was a story of more woe
   Than crushing on a boy who doesn't know.

   What other rhyming couplets can you come up with to describe this book?

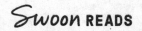

Don't miss Shani Petroff's next
romantic comedy of errors...

My New Crush Gave to Me

You don't need a Christmas miracle
when you have a foolproof plan . . .

Charlotte "Charlie" Donovan knows exactly what she wants for Christmas: Teo Ortiz. He's the school's star athlete, in the National Honor Society, invited to every party, contributes to the school paper (where Charlie is co-editor), and is about to be featured as "One to Watch" in a teen magazine—basically, he's exactly the type of guy Charlie's meant to be with. The only problem—he barely knows she exists.

But Charlie is determined to be Teo's date to the Christmas ball. And she has a plan: to rig the paper's Secret Santa so that she can win his heart with five perfect gifts. But to do that she needs help. Enter J.D. Ortiz—Teo's cousin, and possibly the most annoying person on the planet. He's easygoing, laid-back, unorganized, spontaneous, and makes a joke out of everything —the exact opposite of Charlie (and Teo). But he's willing to provide insight into what Teo wants, so she's stuck with him.

Yet, the more time Charlie spends with J.D., the more she starts to wonder: Does she really know what, or rather who, she wants for Christmas?

*** Coming October 2017 ***

"Today's the day!" I clapped my hands together. "My plan to win over Teo Ortiz officially goes into motion."

Morgan fiddled with the hem of her sweater. "Are you sure you want to go through with this?"

"Of course I'm sure. It's practically all I've been able to think about." I studied her face. "What? Why are you looking at me like that?"

"Like what?" Morgan asked, averting her eyes to the ground.

"Like I'm going to mess this up!"

"I never said that."

"You didn't have to!" That was the thing with a best friend—you knew what was going on in their head, even when you wished you didn't. "This is going to work, I know it."

She gave me that look again.

"What!?" I cried.

"It's just you don't know how to break a rule. Any rule. Are you sure you can do this?"

"I'm not trying to hack into the computer system and change my grades, which FYI, I'm sure I could do if I really wanted, I'm RIGGING A SECRET SANTA drawing." I slapped my hand over my mouth and glanced around the hall to make sure no one else heard me. I was in the clear. "It's not a big deal."

"Says the girl who broke down after taking an extra piece of candy from Mrs. Chevian's doorstep on Halloween."

"I was eight!" I screeched. I regretted ever telling her that story. When I was trick-or-treating in third grade, the Chevians left a bowl of candy on their stoop with a sign that said "take one." I took two, but felt so guilty that by the end of the night I was in tears and went back the next day to apologize.

"Okay, then what about last year, the last day of school?" she asked.

I shrugged. "What about it?"

"Charlie!"

"Fine, yes, everyone who had final period study hall was skipping it to go get pizza. Except for me. I couldn't do it. But this is different. The candy, the cutting class, that was doing something wrong. This isn't. This is for love. And besides," I said, giving her what I hoped was an endearing smile, "you weren't there for either of those things. If you had lived in town when I was in third grade or were in my study hall last year, I would have been fine. But you're here now. Nothing bad is going to happen. I'm sure of it."

She shook her head. "Okay, I'm in. You know that. Let's get you the boy of your dreams."

"Thank you, thank you, thank you," I said and hugged my arms around my chest. This was so going to work.

Morgan may have still had her doubts, but that was okay. I had enough faith for the both of us.

Teo Ortiz was going to have the best Christmas of his life. And so was I. I was going to make sure of it.

Check out more books
chosen for publication
by readers like you.

SHANI PETROFF is a writer living in New York City. She's the author of the Bedeviled series, which includes *Daddy's Little Angel*; *The Good, the Bad, and the Ugly Dress*; *Careful What You Wish For*; and *Love Struck*, and the coauthor of the Destined series, which includes *Ash* and *Ultraviolet*. She also writes for television news programs and several other venues. When she's not locked in her apartment typing away, she spends a whole lot of time on books, boys, TV, daydreaming, and shopping online.

SHANIPETROFF.COM